DEAD MAN'S LEGACY

DEAD MAN'S LEGACY

by

Philip Harbottle

Dales Large Print Books
Long Preston, North Yorkshire,
BD23 4ND, England.

British Library Cataloguing in Publication Data.

Harbottle, Philip
    Dead man's legacy.

        A catalogue record of this book is
        available from the British Library

        ISBN   1-84262-259-5 pbk

First published in Great Britain in 2002 by Robert Hale Limited

Copyright © Philip Harbottle 2002
(Based on a short story by John Russell Fearn)

Cover illustration © Ballestar by arrangement with
Norma Editorial S.A.

Published in Large Print 2003 by arrangement with
Robert Hale Ltd.

Dales Large Print is an imprint of Library Magna Books Ltd.

Printed and bound in Great Britain by
T.J. (International) Ltd., Cornwall, PL28 8RW

1

Evening quiet was upon Henry Farraday's Double G ranch as Sheriff Pat Garson walked heavily up the three veranda steps to the screen door. His big, rosy-checked face was serious. When he came to Farraday's spread it was usually for pleasure – even a game of chess now and again – but this time he was in his official capacity as Sheriff of North Wind Gap.

He thumped heavily on the screen door, and waited. Somewhere round by the stables a collie barked. Then, hazed by the wire, he saw a girl approaching from within: she became clear as she opened the door to him. The long rays of the brassy evening sun livened up blonde hair into golden tints and threw diagonal light on merry grey eyes. Sally Farraday was not quite a beauty, but there was a considerable vivacity and feminine appeal about her.

'Hello, Sheriff.' she greeted. 'Come over to see Dad? Come right in.'

'Thanks, Miss Sally.' Garson smiled at her

rather awkwardly, took off his big hat and followed her graceful figure into a big, comfortable living-room of the usual log-walled variety.

'The sheriff, Dad,' Sally called, going ahead – and a big man with grey hair, open-necked shirt and black riding-breeches got up from a basket chair.

'Howdy, Garson,' he greeted, nodding. 'Always glad to see yuh.'

Her part in the business finished, Sally retired to a far corner by the window and picked up some sewing. Sheriff Garson's dark eyes followed her movements, then he looked back at Farraday.

'I ain't so sure that this ain't private, Farraday...'

'Private!' Henry Farraday raised bushy eyebrows. 'Since when did you and me have private business, Sheriff?'

'Since last night, I reckon.' There was grimness in Garson's tone. He looked as though he didn't like what he was saying.

Farraday looked at him in puzzlement. Tall, austere in expression, he had the hooked nose and high cheekbones of the Indians from whom he was remotely descended. Eyes of cobalt-blue studied the sheriff intently.

'Look here, Garson,' he said finally, 'whatever you an' me have got to talk about ain't so personal that my daughter can't hear it. You'll say your piece right here an' now afore her, or yuh won't say nothin'. Sorry, but my gal an' me don't have no secrets from each other. Now, take a seat. Have a cigar.'

Garson hesitated, then he shrugged and sat down, taking a long black weed from the box Farraday held towards him. Farraday struck a match and his eyes were still mystified over the dancing flame. Then he settled down in the basket-chair again, crossed long, thin legs with their well-polished riding-boots.

'Now, Sheriff, what's eatin' yuh?' he asked bluntly.

'I'll come straight to it, Farraday,' Garson said. 'Jack Andrews came here last night, didn't he?'

'Uh-huh,' Farraday agreed, nodding. 'To see me about some cattle. Why?'

'He ain't been seen since! It's known by 'most everybody that he was comin' here because he told it to his pals down at the Blue Dollar – but since then there's been no trace nor sign o' him. He came here on foot, you not being so far outa town an' he ain't skipped neither because his best horses are

9

still in the stable. Seems like he vanished between leavin' you and walkin' home after dark last night.'

Cobalt-blue eyes sharpened behind cigar smoke.

'What's that to do with me, Garson?'

Garson shrugged. 'Just this, Farraday. I'm your friend, and I reckon you know it. The folks in town is sayin' that you know what happened to Jack Andrews. Some is even sayin' that you dry-gulched him and have hidden the body somewheres. It's well known you an' him were rivals in the cattle-tradin' business, just as it's well known you're one of the richest men in the business. One man stood to queer your pitch – Jack Andrews. So, as friend an' sheriff I'm givin' you the chance to tell me, open like, what you did with him.'

Farraday smiled sourly and knocked the ash from his cigar.

'You're plumb off trail, Sheriff! Jack Andrews left here at a quarter after nine last night an' I saw him go. We only had a short business talk. My gal here can verify it ... that he left, I mean.'

'That's right,' Sally said, her sewing in her lap and her face troubled.

'An' you ain't got no idea where he went?' Garson demanded.

'Far as I know he went home,' Farraday responded. 'That's what he told me, and it was the last I saw o' him... An' I don't like yuh bustin' in here and tellin' me I as good as dry-gulched him! I know my rights, Garson, and you're tramplin' on 'em!'

The sheriff contemplated his cigar. 'You know what this town is, Farraday,' he said finally. 'Jack Andrews was a mighty popular guy around here – and you ain't that exactly. There's a lot o' the brighter spirits in town just waitin' for a chance to put you on the spot. If you don't start talkin' I don't see how I can hold 'em back.'

Farraday got to his feet, stern and cold. He threw his cigar in the empty fireplace.

'Do you think I *did* kill Jack Andrews?' he asked with slow bitterness.

'Nope.' Garson looked up at him steadily. 'I know you well enough to take your word, Farraday ... but I've my duty to do. As the last man to see Jack Andrews alive, and coming nightfall too, you looks mighty suspicious! 'Specially as it would help you a lot to be rid o' him...' Garson got up and tapped Farraday emphatically on his broad chest. 'Get this, Farraday! I can't arrest you on suspicion of murder without Jack Andrew's body being found, but that's becos

11

I've got the law to respect. The rest of the boys around North Wind mightn't be so particklar. As a straight tip, either admit what you did and let me lock you safely behind bars ... or else get outa here, an' quick! And take Miss Sally with you.'

Farraday smiled crookedly. 'I c'n take care of myself, Garson! But I c'n see what you're gettin' at. Yuh mean lynch law still operates, eh?'

'Yeah. I'm only one man with a handful of underlings. We ain't strong enough to stop an organized neck-tie party,'

Farraday shrugged broad shoulders and the muscles tightened in his face.

'I c'n take what's comin', Sheriff, and I'll blow the feet off the first dirty cowpuncher that sets foot unlawfully on my territory!' He patted the sixgun strapped low on his thigh. 'Thanks fer tippin' me off though ... but I don't know anythin' about Jack Andrews runnin' out, and I ain't runnin' out neither!'

Garson hesitated, then he swept his big hat back on to his crimped brown hair.

'OK, Farraday, I'll take your word for it– But for gosh sakes look out for yourself! 'Night! 'Night, Miss Sally.'

The girl nodded vaguely after him, then

she got to her feet and hurried over to where her father was standing, two fingers tapping the butt of his sixgun, his thin proud lips tightly compressed.

'Dad ... what are you going to do?'

He started from preoccupation and smiled down at her.

'Stay right here, lass, o' course. My own conscience is clear enough, an' no man who's worth anythin' runs out unless he's done somethin'! You know Jack Andrew left here safe an' sound last night and we don't need to know any more'n that!'

Sally gave a little shiver. 'But, Dad, some of the boys in town won't look at it that way! Just as the sheriff said, this Jack Andrews mystery may be genuine or it may be a put-up job to make things tough for you. You're too strong to get at in the ordinary way and that's why most of 'em hate you. Being the owner of the Grey Face mine doesn't help your case any either. It makes it look as though you've got everything and the rest nothing.'

'I've everythin' I need, anyway,' Farraday said, putting an arm round the girl's shoulders. 'A good business, a gal who's been eddicated and who's a rare housekeeper for me...' He stopped and shrugged. 'How it

13

looks, lass, an' how it is are two different things. I've made money outa cattle trading, sure … but as fer that mine I never made anythin' outa it. It hardly paid me back fer the labour I put into it. That's why I ain't touched it for ten year an' more... As fer the boys in town gettin' restive, don't you git aworryin' yerself. I c'n look after the both of us.'

The girl made no answer. Since returning from Glover City where she had completed her education she had often been secretly appalled by the lawlessness of North Wind Gap.

The Blue Dollar Saloon was at the height of the evening's business when the gathering human storm showed signs of breaking. Boyd Wilcot sensed it the moment he'd left his tethered dun and entered the batwings into the smoky interior. He was a medium-sized man of about fifty, immaculately dressed in a black suit, snowy-white shirt, and a gambler's shoestring tie. Fine dust blurred the shine on his glossy riding-boots and filmed the black sombrero he pushed up on his wide forehead.

Twin guns slapping low on his thighs from cross-over belts, he went to the bar, ordered

14

whiskey, then turned dark, pensive eyes to the assembly. For some reason he smiled to himself.

Offhand, everything looked normal enough. The cowpunchers of North Wind Gap were seated before their drinks or playing cards; others were busy at the poker-layouts and pool-tables. A faded blonde standing nearby under a small hanging tub of bright flowers was trying to infuse red-hot rhythm into a threadbare song as a pianist plugged it savagely. In a far corner near a staircase which led to his office the oily-haired, swarthily good-looking Clem Billings was chewing a cheroot and no doubt mentally assessing the dollars building up to his credit. The Blue Dollar saloon had been good to him in the past five years.

Yes, it was a typical evening, on the surface – but Boyd Wilcot knew of certain things under the surface. He knew the place inside out and most of the men who frequented it. Many of them indeed were his own employees. At last he set down his emptied glass and strolled across the smoky room, rolling a cigarette as he went. By the time he had reached the side of Clem Billings he had it lighted in a corner of his thin-lipped mouth.

15

'Something's brewing here tonight, Clem.' Wilcot spoke with perfect enunciation, his eyes moving over the busy scene. 'I can sense it.'

'Not surprised,' Clem grunted, dusting ash from his fancy waistcoat. 'You've heard about Jack Andrews, ain't you?'

'That he's probably been murdered? Yes, I heard.'

Clem tightened his pointed chin. 'There don't seem much doubt about it to me, Wilcot, that he's been bushwhacked an' his body hidden. There's only one man in town who might ha' had reason to do it – Henry Farraday.'

'He's not that kind of man,' Wilcot replied, shaking his head.

'You'll say that, of course!' Clem flashed him a contemptuous glance. 'You're his best friend. You an' him is about on a par when it comes to money. You got the Treble Circle spread from your father and all the money that went with it, and you got education as a gent back East. Farraday fought his way to the top without education and used a gold-mine an' cattle to do it with. That's the only difference, but you both sit pretty.'

'You sound as if you don't like men who've got money,' Wilcot murmured, smiling.

'Can't think why: you're not exactly poor yourself. You own this saloon and several shops in town, and you've told me you're hoping to expand into ranching eventually...'

'I ain't sayin' anything of the sort. It's just Farraday I don't like. Too bossy! Never comes in here and drinks like other guys. Never gambles. That sorta man is just plain, stinking ornery to my way of thinkin'. That daughter of his is a nice looker, I'll grant. But she's under his thumb, so we hardly see her in here either. Pity...' he broke off, realizing he was drifting. Then: 'I think Farraday *did* murder Jack Andrews and I'm all for gettin' the truth outa him and to hell with the law!'

Wilcot seemed to hesitate over a thought, then he drew off his gloves slowly and slapped them across his palm. He had barely done it before the spurious calm over the saloon's proceedings suddenly exploded. A cowpuncher, small but muscle-packed, leapt up on to the bar counter and waved his hands over his head. The men at the tables sat looking at him expectantly.

'Hey, Curly, kill that goddamned piano!' the man shouted – and Curly obliged, bony fingers dropping to his knees.

The faded blonde folded plump bare arms

and waited boredly. Wilcot narrowed his dark eyes a little, a curious look of expectancy on his handsome face.

'That's Shorty Cartwright on the counter, isn't it?' he asked Clem.

'Yeah. Jack Andrews' right-hand man.'

'How much longer do we sit around here and kid ourselves?' Shorty demanded, thumbs hooked on his gun belt as he addressed the men. 'We're all itchin' on the trigger finger to do just one thing – drag Farraday into the open and beat the truth outa him! I saw the Sheriff afore I came in here tonight and he ain't doin' nothin' to Farraday becos he reckons there's nobody to prove what happened. I say that ain't no way to git the truth out of a guy like Farraday! He's as hard as rock and tricky as a coyote. We all know he hated my boss Jack Andrews – and we all know it would be better for Farraday with my boss outa the way.'

There was a mumbling of assent from the assembled men.

'Jack Andrews were my boss,' Shorty repeated, 'an' if anythin' has happened to him I reckon it's my job to find out what and not wait fer Sheriff Garson to go huntin' for proofs. Plenty of youse fellers here knew and liked Jack Andrews. How many of yuh is with me in beatin' the truth outa Farraday?'

Confusion rocked several tables as a number of men sprang to their feet. Others remained seated and grimly silent. Wilcot and Clem watched for a moment, then Wilcot settled his sombrero in its normal position on his head.

'See you later,' he said briefly, and went off without a word of explanation, watched by Clem's coldly suspicious eyes.

Walking behind the men shouting at the bar Wilcot made his way through the batwings and out into the street. It was a couple of hours after sundown now and there were only the lights over the high street and from one or two stores casting an uncertain glow.

In a few seconds he had reached his horse tethered to the boardwalk rail. The moment he was in the saddle the dun started forward at a touch of the spur, fled with high, fast steps into the night. Wilcot made his journey swiftly, leaving a trail of dust behind him, drawing rein finally outside the Farraday ranch, a patchwork of grey and white in the rising moonlight.

He tied the reins to the corral gate and

hurried over to the shadowy veranda and banged fiercely on the screen door.

It was Farraday himself who opened it – a tall dim figure with the moonlight glinting on the sixgun in his right hand.

'It's me, Wilcot,' Wilcot said breathlessly. 'Let me in, quick!'

'Boyd!' Farraday opened the door wider and then relocked it, preceding Wilcot into the living-room. Sally was there, standing somewhat taut and strained.

'Evening, Sally,' Wilcot said briefly, taking his sombrero from his glossy dark hair; then he swung back to Farraday. 'The boys are out gunning for you, Henry! They're mostly on foot, I think. I came by horse to get here ahead of them. They'll be here any minute. I was in the Blue Dollar when they had a powwow to decide to get some action out of you. They're all sure you killed Jack Andrews.'

'Yeah, I know.' Farraday twirled his gun in strong fingers. 'But I ain't gettin' off my own property fer nobody, Boyd! An' there ain't no call fer yuh to take such a risk comin' to warn me.'

'Forget it! I'm your friend. And I'm telling you to get out, man! You can't fight a mob of men single-handed, and besides plenty of them have had too much to drink. They've no real idea what they're doing. Why don't you and Sally here hit the trail, at least until morning?'

Farraday shook his head with Indian impassiveness. 'I stay!'

Wilcot raised his gloved hands and let them fall back helplessly to his sides, then he looked up sharply as a sound came out of the night. It was the lowing of cattle on the move.

The lines round Farraday's mouth tightened harshly. He swung to the window and raised the shade. For a moment or two he gazed outside and then exploded in fury.

'The dirty no-account buzzards!' he shouted. 'They're drivin' my cattle out of the corral to God knows where. Drivin' 'em out with torches, too. Hell, this isn't gettin' at me! It's just plain smashin' up my business instead...!'

He strode towards the living-room door and half opened it, then he swung back as a bullet whanged through the lighted window and shattered the glass.

'Down!' Wilcot snapped, and flung Sally flat on her face to the floor.

Farraday extinguished the light and crept back to the window, his sixgun in his hand.

Out there in the moonlight he could see his precious cattle on the move, stampeding before waving torches and shifting men. There was the crackle of guns, shouts – then another bullet splintered through the window and split the mirror on the other side of the room.

'Damn it, if I could only see who's firin',' Farraday breathed, his voice half-stifled with fury.

'Probably Shorty Cartwright,' Wilcot said briefly, his own gun in his hand as he inched towards the window. 'Maybe we can... Say, they're setting fire to the place!' He broke off in alarm.

There was no doubt of it. The barns and stables had begun to spout sparks and smoke. Glowing drifts were moving on the still night air towards the ranch house itself. To Farraday's bitter eyes the whole thing now looked like some crazy patchwork of swirling torches, pounding cattle, and the pulsing beat of flame.

'Where are your boys, anyway?' Wilcot demanded. 'Aren't there enough of them to keep this sort of thing in hand?'

'They're in town,' Farraday muttered. 'Nothin' much to do after sundown–' He stopped and swung violently as the living-room door crashed open.

'Reach, Farraday!' ordered a cold voice. 'You're covered – and so is your gal. One false move from you and she gets it – pronto!'

Farraday straightened and dropped his gun to the floor. It was Shorty Cartwright who stood in the doorway, clearly visible now as the flames outside gathered flickering brilliance. In each of his hands was a six-shooter, steadily levelled.

'You too, Wilcot!' he snapped, as Wilcot got up slowly from his knees beside the window. 'Drop your gun!'

2

Very slowly Boyd Wilcot obeyed. Shorty waited as Farraday, Sally and then Wilcot raised their hands to shoulder level and kept them there.

'It's you we want Farraday,' Shorty went on, hardly moving his lips. 'Come out on to the porch here – an' don't try no tricks. We got everythin' just the way we want it, see, and your own boys is being taken care of too, so don't expect any help from 'em.'

The guns motioned silently. Farraday, grim-faced, walked past Shorty slowly and out on to the porch. Outside, as he stood with fingers clenching the wood rail, he could see a knot of men, illuminated clearly by the spreading fire.

'I'll just wise yuh up to what we figger on doin', Farraday,' Shorty said. 'Sheriff Garson's gone sour on us waitin' for proofs of Jack Andrews' death, but we don't reckon to wait. We could ha' made this a necktie party but that'd probably get us all in a spot with the law – so we've decided to run yuh out o' town instead! The hard way! An' we're burnin' down your spread an' turnin' all your cattle loose, or mebbe we'll make use of 'em ourselves later,' Shorty added, with a grim smile.

'When Sheriff Garson gets to hear of this–' Wilcot began, but Shorty cuffed him viciously across the face.

'Shut up, you! Think yerself lucky you don't get run outa town too for sidin' up with this guy Farraday. All right, boys, *take him!*'

Shorty swung Farraday fiercely to one side and then shoved him stumbling down the steps. Immediately he was seized and thrown on his face in the dust while his wrists were firmly tied behind him.

'What – what are you going to do?' Sally gasped, her eyes wide.

'Give your gun-shootin' pop the ride of his life,' Shorty told her briefly. 'Don't fret; you're goin to see it from close quarters cos you're goin with him! Right, boys, take the girl an' dump her in the saddle!'

Protesting and struggling Sally was forced down the steps, raised in strong hands into the saddle of a restive horse. Before she grasped what was happening her wrists were secured crosswise to the saddle horn and her ankles to the stirrups. She turned her head and watched fixedly. Her father was lying on his back now, his ankles tied together and a length of rope trailing to the back of the saddle on which she sat. Once the horse started going...!

'You can't do this, you idiot!' Wilcot raved. 'This isn't a run-out! It's plain murder! And look at the fire!'

Ignoring him Shorty swaggered down the steps, went over to the prostrate Farraday and kicked him in the ribs.

'If either of yuh come back it'll be jus' too bad!' he said slowly. 'Now git goin'!'

He slapped the flat of his hand on the

25

horse's twitching flank and with the other hand fired his revolver into the air. Startled, the beast lunged forward and tore blindly towards the open gateway in the moonlight, streaked through it and away from the doomed ruin of ranch and stables.

'Dad! Dad, *I can't stop him!*' Sally shrieked, tearing frantically but uselessly at her bound hands.

Maddened by the weight of the man he was dragging across the rough scrub behind him the horse snorted and thundered onwards under the stars and moon. Farraday felt the razor edges of grass bite into his flesh; rough stones pounded his face and bound hands. He was half-blinded with dust from the horse's racing hoofs. Sally dragged at her wrists until blood showed beneath the ropes but she was powerless to budge them in the slightest. Her feet she dare not move in case she accidentally spurred the beast to even wilder frenzy.

Within a few minutes the flames of the burning ranch had become hidden by a rise in the ground. The horse was stampeding well off-trail now across open country, stumbling in scrub and loose sandy soil. Glancing back, Sally could not see her father now. Dust hazed him but she could feel the sickening jolts from the horse beneath her as her father's body was dragged and battered through the merciless earth.

At last she screamed. It was the only thing she could do in her extremity. It was a scream of fear, of anguish, a desperate cry for help to the bright stars and mellow moon. It eased her somehow and she then tried to call the horse to a halt. But it failed to respond. It was not one of the Double G beasts anyway but a rather mangy-looking horse that Shorty Cartwright had evidently brought specially for the purpose. So Sally had no luck and it raced onwards with her knees pressed into its sweating sides.

Then presently Sally caught a new sound – the thunder of hoofs other than those of the horse to which she was tied. She glanced over her shoulder but only saw that mushroom of dust. But the pounding hoofs were coming nearer and nearer still, until at last a horseman loomed out of the haze and moonlight, drew level, then reached out and caught at the bridle of the runaway. He tugged, he pulled, he struggled. Snorting and panting the runaway dragged gradually to a standstill and pawed fretfully as steam rose from its neck.

The stranger dismounted – a tall, spare figure clearly visible in the moonlight. Behind him another horseman came up, drew rein, and jumped to the ground. He was a much shorter man, also a stranger to Sally.

Half fainting, the girl dragged free her bleeding wrists as a keen knife slashed the rope. Then her ankles were freed. Strong hands under her arms lifted her gently to the ground.

'My – my father...' she whispered, swaying giddily. 'He's – back there...'

'I know.' The stranger's voice was quiet, resourceful. 'Take hold of her, Bill: she's still a bit woozy.'

The shorter man slipped his arm round Sally's waist and grinned at her faintly from under a broad-brimmed hat. She murmured her thanks, then stumbled forward to where her father was lying prostrate in the dust. The knife-blade flashed and the ropes fell away. The stranger turned Farraday over, peered at him, felt his heart.

'Is – is he...?' Sally's voice sounded far away.

'I reckon he's unconscious, but still alive,' the stranger said. 'Badly knocked about as you might expect, but his heart's regular.

Leave this to me.'

He hauled the limp form of Farraday on to a broad shoulder, walked with him to the horse he had been riding and laid him carefully over the saddle.

'Bill, you ride the runaway,' he ordered. 'Miss, you come with me on my horse. Up you get!'

He lifted her with consummate ease to the saddle of the horse Bill had been riding, then vaulted up behind her. Reining in his own mare with Farraday lying limply across it he set the animal moving at a jog-trot beside him.

'What no-account skunk did this to yuh?' Bill demanded, peering at Sally in the moonlight.

'I was about to ask the same thing, miss,' said the other, into her ear. 'Lucky for you that Bill an' me heard you screaming. We'd just been over to Glover City to fix up some business and were on our way home... Say, I'm sorta fergetting! I'm Ken Bradmore, owner of the Straight H. It's about six miles from here. This is my foreman, Bill Winslow.'

'Howdy,' Bill murmured, touching his hat.

'It's all so horrible,' Sally muttered, running a bloodstained hand through her thick hair. 'We – my dad and I – were driven out of town and our ranch was burned down and the cattle stampeded. We're from North Wind Gap.'

'North Wind, huh?' Ken Bradmore ruminated as they jogged along. 'Yeah, that's a few miles from here, isn't it – beside the mountain trail? Tough little burg without much respect for law 'n order, from what I've heard. But what did your pop do to get a farewell party like this?'

'They think he murdered a man.' Sally's voice was low. 'But he didn't! Really he didn't, Mr Bradmore! I – er... Oh, it's too awful to talk about!'

'Then don't,' Ken said in sympathy. 'We'll have a chin about it when you've rested up a bit.'

Thereafter they rode in virtual silence, until at length the little party came to the top of a rise.

'There's my spread,' Ken said, pointing ahead.

Sally looked, and across the moonlit pastureland saw the yellow gleam of lights from unshaded windows and the dim outlines of extensive cattle enclosures.

'My sister keeps house for me,' Ken added. 'You'll like Emmy; she can't never do enough for folk – 'specially when they're in distress, like you and your pop.'

An hour later Sally was beginning to feel more comfortable. Her father had been put to bed and the doctor had been summoned from the nearby town in Waterfall Valley – and had departed. Farraday was badly lacerated and bruised, and he had broken his left arm – but he was anything but dead. Iron-hard physique and a rip-snorting desire for revenge would no doubt put him back on his feet in double-quick time. At the moment he was sound asleep. This knowledge more than anything else brought ease of mind back to Sally.

She sat now in the roomy basket-chair in the living-room of the Bradmore ranch. She had met Ken's younger sister Emily, buxom and flaxen-haired, a good-natured soul who obviously enjoyed making other folk happy, and now she had her first chance to properly appraise her rescuers.

Ken Bradmore was in his early thirties; raw-boned, well over six feet, with twin Colts at each thigh. He talked with a faint, slow drawl, but behind the cold grey eyes and firm mouth there was action aplenty going on. Underneath that untidy black hair there was anything but the brain of a sluggard.

Bill Winslow was different stuff; short, dressed in the conventional cowpuncher's outfit, with one hand usually resting on his gun butt as though he expected trouble. Doubtless he was a good foreman and a loyal sidekick, but although he was about the same age as Ken, he didn't register in the same way ... sandy haired, round faced... Sally's attention diverted itself automatically to the vaguely diffident Ken.

By degrees, as she drank the coffee Emily had brought her, Sally got her story out. Ken Bradmore paced about restlessly as she talked, pondering, his brows low over his keen grey eyes. At last he nodded, drew a chair up beside the girl and angled his bony figure into it.

'Look here, Miss Farraday, what was Sheriff Garson doin' to allow that sorta thing to happen?'

'He couldn't have stopped it,' Sally said seriously. 'No sheriff can break mob law.'

'Mmmm, mebbe.' Ken considered the fact for a moment. Then: 'And your friend, Boyd Wilcot, who brought the warning. What happened to him?'

'I just don't know; everything happened so fast. Last I saw of him was when Shorty Cartwright hit him across the face for talking out of turn.'

'I've seen him before,' Ken said slowly 'Medium-sized, stiff-built fellow, near middle age, always well dressed... Yes, seen him before in Glover City many a time.'

'He's quite the wealthiest man in North Wind,' Sally said. 'And it may account for Shorty and his trigger-men not doing very much to him.'

'Your pop ain't exactly without money, either...' The grey eyes were thoughtful. 'At least he wasn't until everything was stampeded – yet Shorty and his boys ran *him* out of town. An' with no proof that he ever killed Jack Andrews either! Sounds to me, Miss Farraday, as though there's somethin' screwy somewheres, if you git my meanin'. Just as though Shorty and the others wanted to break your pop's business power more than anything else. Otherwise, why did they burn down your spread and stampede your cattle? That sorta smells like an effort to drive you and your pop into liquidation.'

'And a highly successful effort, too,' Sally sighed. 'Dad's business literally went up in flames tonight, Mr Bradmore. He was one of the biggest cattle men in North Wind before tonight. Of course he has savings and securities in the Glover City bank, but when your business has been destroyed it means using your capital, and that's bad in any language. And Dad won't be able to get things moving again for some time, judging from the mess he's in.'

Ken ran a finger along the side of his jaw. 'Look here – this Shorty Cartwright. He was Andrews' sidekick, you say?'

'That's right. Has a bit of a dirty history, too. He was an owlhooter once. Some questionable business with the Glover City stage but he wriggled out of it with Jack Andrews' help and a shyster lawyer to pull the strings.'

'I'm just thinkin' that he seemed mighty anxious to avenge the death of his boss,' Ken said, musing. 'Sorta queer to my way of figgerin'... Right-hand men aren't *that* anxious, as a rule; not Shorty's type anyway. Like as not he'd be more inclined to take up where his boss left off. Any chance that he took orders from somebody?'

Sally reflected, then shook her blonde head. 'I don't think so – unless Clem Billings had something to do with it. He's the owner of the Blue Dollar saloon,' she explained, seeing Ken's glance. 'He hates my dad because he made his money the straight way. As a saloon-owner Clem isn't so particular.'

'Mmm...' Ken got to his feet and glanced across at Bill's comfortable, lounging form. 'Any notions, Bill?'

'Sounds like a plumb loco setup to me,' Bill decided. 'I reckon I never heard tell of an overheated mob behavin' so – so sorta organized. More like it were planned, for a reason.'

'Just what I'm thinking.' Ken smiled widely down at the girl. 'I think Bill and me can spare the time for a trot into North Wind tomorrow, Miss Farraday. There's a few things I want to get straightened out in my mind. Think that way, too Bill?'

'Yeah.' Bill glanced at Emily and noted her approving smile. He nodded his sandy head. 'I reckon so, boss.'

It was early morning when Ken Bradmore and Bill trotted their horses into the dusty high street of North Wind Gap the following day. On the way they had passed the blackened ruin of Farraday's ranch and the vision of it had hardened the lines in Ken Bradmore's face.

Now, as he drew rein, he looked about him. The town was passing busy. Women were coming in and out of the stores, cowpunchers came and went. Now and again a buckboard and team came rattling through.

'Seems to me,' Ken said presently, turning hard grey eyes on Bill, 'that somebody in this dust-caked burg has a mighty powerful grudge against old man Farraday and the girl – and I'm not quite sure where to start rootin'. I reckon we might do worse 'n see this guy Clem Billings. Come on.'

They rode further down the street, dismounted outside the Blue Dollar and tied their horses to the boardwalk rail. When they got into the saloon they found it empty, in the process of being cleaned out. The shirt-sleeved bartender nodded to the staircase at the far end when Ken had made his mission clear.

'Yeah, you'll find the boss in. Go straight through, gents.'

Ken nodded and mounted the staircase with Bill behind him. They found the slick-haired Clem behind a roll-top desk, thumbing through a wad of bills.

'Well, gents?' he asked presently, turning and brushing cheroot ash from his fancy waistcoat. 'What c'n I do for you?'

Ken cuffed up his hat on his forehead and half straddled a chair. 'Ever hear of Henry Farraday?' he asked briefly, his grey eyes fixing on the dark ones.

Clem gave an easy nod. 'Sure. He and his daughter were driven outa town last night. And I mean driven!'

'Why?' Ken asked, his voice cold.

'Fer pluggin' a guy named Jack Andrews an' then hidin' the body. Law couldn't touch him so some of the boys did. They get outa hand around here sometimes...' Clem's expression slowly changed and he sat up. 'Why, what's it to you, stranger?'

'I'm just lookin' for Farraday, that's all,' Ken replied. 'I heard a different story – that he was driven out of town on your orders. That Shorty Cartwright did the whole thing on your say-so.'

Clem leapt to his feet, his hand jumping to his holster. But Ken stood up too, twin Colts already levelled.

'Don't do it,' he advised calmly. 'We can talk this over like gentlemen, I reckon. Now let me get something straight, mister. How much did it help you to get Farraday out of town?'

'It didn't help me!' Clem retorted.

'Yeah, but you didn't like him, did you? Because he's a square shooter – an' you, like most of the ten-cent heels in this town – are not.'

37

'Of course I don't like him, chiefly because I never made any money outa him. He never came in my saloon, never even took no notice of me. But he could either come or go as far as I'm concerned. I'm a saloon-owner – doin' well – not a cattle man. Why should I want to rub out Farraday? What'd it get me?'

'Come to think of it, boss, why should he?' Bill murmured. 'If any guy'd be afraid of Farraday it'd be a cattleman, the way I figger it. Mebbe Shorty *did* think it all up by himself at that.'

'Ex-owl-hooters haven't that much brain,' Ken growled; then he suddenly holstered his Colts and nodded. 'Okay, Clem, I think you're on the level,' he decided. 'Let's go, Bill.'

Clem stood staring after them somewhat blankly as they left the office. When they got out to the street again Ken halted and pondered.

'Either he's a mighty good actor or he had nothing to do with this,' he said finally. 'Best thing we can do is try and find Shorty himself and beat some sense outa him. Then we–'

'Say, ain't that Wilcot?' Bill interrupted, nodding down the high street. 'It's the guy we've seen in Glover City, leastways.'

Ken turned and studied an immaculate lone horseman in the distance, watering his horse at the trough.

'It's Wilcot all right,' Ken agreed. 'Might have a word with him.'

In a few moments' easy riding they had drawn up alongside Wilcot as he stood beside the trough. As usual he was faultlessly dressed in his black suit, white shirt, and broad-brimmed sombrero.

'Howdy,' Ken greeted amiably, leaning on his saddle horn.

Wilcot glanced up with surprised dark eyes. Then he nodded a trifle vaguely. 'Howdy,' Wilcot acknowledged. 'Ought I to know you two gentlemen?'

'I'm Ken Bradmore of the Straight H down in Waterfall Valley. This is Bill Winslow, my cattle foreman.' The introduction over, Ken asked, 'You're Mr Boyd Wilcot, I think? I've seen you around Glover City now and again.'

'Supposing I am?'

'As Henry Farraday's best friend you might be interested in knowin' he and his daughter are both at my ranch. Bill and me picked 'em up last night after that drive-out they got.'

Wilcot's expression changed abruptly from suspicion to eagerness. 'Then – then they weren't killed?' he asked quickly.

'Nope. The old man's got a broken arm and the helluva lot of bruises and the girl's got grazed wrists.'

'Thank heaven it was no worse! I've been wondering what had happened to them – and as a matter of fact I was just off to make a search for them. That's why I'm watering my horse. Since you know where they are it makes it easier. I'll come back to your ranch with you, if I may...'

'Nothing to stop you doin' that, I reckon,' Ken agreed. 'Only...'

'Well?' Wilcot questioned.

'Just that I've a bit of unfinished business yet, Mr Wilcot. Tell you what: meet me outside the Blue Dollar in fifteen minutes.'

'Suit me nicely,' Wilcot agreed. 'I've one or two calls to make myself anyway.'

3

As they trotted up the street again Bill aimed an enquiring eye at Ken. 'What's next, boss?'

'The sheriff. I want to find out why he hasn't done anything about that business last night. There's his office over there. Wait for me.'

Bill nodded and Ken dismounted, strode up the steps and into the sheriffs office. He found him at his desk looking over some correspondence.

'Howdy,' he said glancing up.

'I don't rightly know whether I should return that greeting or not, Sheriff,' Ken said slowly, resting strong hands on the desk and gazing at Garson pensively. 'I want to know what sort of a town you're runnin' here when a man past middle age and a girl in her twenties can get beaten outa town the hard way, an' have their ranch burned and cattle stampeded. Or mebbe North Wind Gap ain't so particular when it comes to laws?'

'What's your interest in this?' Garson asked briefly.

'The fact that I picked up Farraday and his girl last night and they told me what happened. Don't tell me that you don't know who roused those hoodlums, Sheriff; it was Shorty Cartwright.'

'Can you prove it?' Garson demanded.

'Well, no. Just hearsay, I reckon.'

'Then it's time you realized the law can't take heed of hearsay! 'Course I know who did it, but when one half the boys are on Cartwright's side and the others are too doggone yeller to let their hair down and talk straight before a court o' law, where am I? Even the Mounties have been beaten before today because of no proof. That's how I am.'

'You mean you couldn't get anybody to testify that Shorty began that run-out?'

'Just that. Farraday's own men are scared of parking lead in their insides if they say too much, and unless I can get at least two witnesses who ain't scared I can't do nothin'. The shootin'-irons are doin' the talkin' in North Wind at present.'

'An' you didn't send out a posse or anything to look for Farraday and his girl?'

'I *did* – but I couldn't find 'em. Now you

say you've got 'em that's one responsibility less. How are Farraday and the girl, by the way?'

Ken told him, then added slowly, 'Look here, Sheriff, Farraday tells me he was run outa town for a murder he didn't commit. Is that the way you figger it, too?'

'It's the only way I can figger it, stranger.'

'Suppose it was for somethin' else? Suppose the disappearance of Jack Andrews just happens to make a mighty convenient cover-up?'

Garson frowned. 'I don't get it. What other reason could there be?'

'I dunno; that's why I'm askin' you – and gettin' no place mighty fast, I reckon. Can you tell me what enemies Farraday has in this town?'

'Most everybody really – exceptin' myself. They're a tough bunch here, stranger, and they're kind of naturally inborn suspicious of a man who makes a pile honestly, as Farraday has. Then his high an' mighty manner didn't make him exactly the sociable type. For myself, I've always found him as square a shooter as ever held a sixgun... As far as big-shot enemies are concerned I c'n think of only two – Clem Billings of the Blue Dollar, and the vanished

Jack Andrews. He was a tidy big cattle man.'

'Uh-huh. I've heard about him. In fact I've seen him knockin' around Glover City now and again just as I've seen Mr Wilcot. He's a big cattle man too?'

'Yeah,' Garson acknowledged. 'Him, Andrews, and Farraday sorta made three of 'em hereabouts.'

'And Clem Billings is not a cattle man,' Luke mused, his grey eyes slitting. 'Something's beginning to make sense in my mind, Sheriff. Look here, if I can bring you any definite proof of who did kill Jack Andrews – if he's dead – can you use it?'

'Can I!' Garson exclaimed. 'Get me one scrap of proof – real, solid proof – and I'll act faster than dynamite. An' to somethin' else while we're at it. Don't let Farraday or his gal turn up again in this town until things are straight. Too unhealthy for 'em.'

'I'll remember,' Ken promised, straightening up. 'And thanks for everything. Sorry I sounded a bit raw. Be seein' you again before long mebbe.'

Ken departed briskly and returned to his horse outside. Bill gave him an inquiring glance as they rode up the street towards the Blue Dollar where Boyd Wilcot was waiting for them on his mouse-coloured dun.

44

'Dig anythin' out o' the sheriff, boss?' Bill asked.

'Mebbe. Right now I'm just interested in one fact – that Farraday, Wilcot and Andrews made up the three biggest cattlemen in this town. I'm just tryin' to figger if it all adds up. Howdy, Mr Wilcot,' Ken broke off, raising a hand in greeting. 'Are we ready?'

'And waiting,' Wilcot agreed, smiling.

He rode between Ken and Bill as they struck the trail outside the town and headed up-country for Waterfall Valley.

'Known Farraday long?' Ken asked casually, as they went along.

'Nearly twenty years.' Wilcot held the reins lightly in his gloved hands. 'I came to North Wind Gap from San Francisco just about a year after him. His daughter Sally was only a small child then and he'd just lost his wife with a fever... We've been very good friends – and will go on being so, I trust.'

'Then you can still be good friends though you're both in the cattle business?' Ken asked.

'There's a difference between us which keeps us friendly,' Wilcot said, smiling. 'I inherited my ranch and cattle business from my father. I came out here to take it over, found I liked the life, and so decided to keep the business going. But I don't *have* to do it, understand! I have financial interests over in 'Frisco which will keep me on easy street until the day I die. It isn't that way with Farraday. He lives or dies by cattle – but with never having had any need to cut his throat in order to save my business we've become the best of friends. Unlike Jack Andrews. He too lived – or lives – by cattle. If he really did die it means that Farraday has no rival, since he doesn't need to fear me.'

'Farraday's ranch and cattle have gone,' Ken said grimly. 'How do you figger Farraday's goin' to keep his business?'

'I've an idea about that,' Wilcot said. 'That's one reason why I'm coming with you now.'

'Look, Mr Wilcot,' Bill said, 'do you reckon Farraday dry-gulched Andrews to remove opposition to his cattle business?'

Wilcot shrugged immaculate shoulders. 'It's possible, of course. Farraday is a tough, rugged character and he might have thought it worth his while to remove a dangerous business competitor, but somehow I can't think it of him.'

Ken said nothing further. His cold grey

46

eyes were narrowed in pursuit of an inner thought.

When they arrived in the Bradmore living-room they found to their surprise that Farraday himself was seated in the basket-chair, his left arm heavily bandaged and set in a sling, with more wrappings around his body, and plasters over one half of his face. Sally was standing close to him and Emily was feeding him something steaming from a basin.

'Well, what happened here?' Ken exclaimed blankly, coming forward. 'On the move so soon, Mr Farraday?'

'I'm not an infant,' Farraday growled, glaring with his one visible blue eye. 'I got the heebie-jeebies sittin' in bed with these durned cheesecloths wrapped round me. Nothin' like gettin' to your feet if yuh can, and – Boyd!' he broke off in delight, catching sight of Wilcot. 'Hell, I'm sure glad to see yuh safe an' sound– Take this stuff away, woman!' he implored Emily, motioning to the bowl.

She smiled, shrugged, and went out. Wilcot came forward and put his black sombrero down on the table, looked at Farraday critically.

'Well, I'm mighty glad it didn't turn out any worse for you and Sally, Henry,' he said. 'When you'd gone they gave me a rough five minutes – but they let it go at that. Scared maybe of how far the long arm might reach. I debated whether to tell the sheriff about it, but I'd no witnesses I could trust, so I couldn't act.'

Ken rubbed his jaw pensively and watched Wilcot through level grey eyes.

'How much hell-fired damage did those hyenas do?' Farraday demanded.

'The ranch is burned out,' Wilcot told him, sighing. 'I'm really sorry about that. As for your cattle... Well, near as I can tell they were stampeded to the four winds. Most of them will be caught, of course, by Shorty and his boys. They've only to switch brands and... You can guess the rest.'

'An' what's that goddamned sheriff doin'?' Farraday raved. 'What's he wearin' that star for – to keep his chest warm?'

'I've seen him,' Ken put in quietly, perching on the table so he could be nearer Sally. 'He says he can't do nothin' without proof, or else a witness who isn't leary of Shorty.'

'Proof! Proof!' Farraday shouted. 'Th' man carries it to the point o' religion!'

'Not altogether,' Wilcot said, thinking. 'Without proof you can't get very far legally, you know. I can see the dilemma he's in.'

'You knew what Shorty planned to do,' Ken remarked. 'Couldn't you have told the sheriff about it?'

'Certainly,' Wilcot acknowledged. 'I alone, with nobody to verify my statement? It wouldn't have got me very far.'

Ken turned to the contemplation of his boots.

'And no evidence has turned up about Jack Andrews?' Farraday asked, breathing fiercely.

Wilcot shook his head. 'Afraid not. I've a private suspicion myself that Clem Billings is mixed up in all this, but I'll only be able to find out by degrees. I'm working for you on the quiet, Henry, don't you forget it. In the meantime I'd like to offer a bit of practical help. Now your ranch and cattle have gone, how do you stand financially?'

Farraday considered, his jaw grimly set.

'I c'n git by,' he said finally. 'I reckon it'll take pretty nearly all I've got to git my cattle restarted an' a new ranch built – but I'll do it. An' when I've done it I'll spend th' rest o' my life payin' out them hyenas fer what they done to me!'

'I don't blame you,' Wilcot said quietly. 'Anyway, I was talking about practical help. I know you must have made a fair amount of money, but a bit more – just a friendly gesture – might be welcome. You're too stubborn to take a gift, so I'll buy something from you to make the thing easier.'

Ken and Bill exchanged glances across the room. Farraday's blue eyes took on a light of surprise.

'You'll buy somethin' from me?' he repeated. 'But everythin's gone, man! Anyway, how much do you figger yuh want to give me?'

'Five thousand dollars,' Wilcot shrugged. 'That would help you a bit wouldn't it?'

'Sure... But I've nothin' to sell!'

'You have the Grey Face mine, haven't you?'

'*That* hole in the rocks!' Farraday exclaimed. 'Durn it, I haven't worked it fer ten year – an' when I did I got nothin' much outa it but dust an' hard labour. There's no gold in it,' he finished emphatically.

Wilcot smiled enigmatically. 'You gave up working it when you got on well with cattle. I'd like to reopen it. Anyway, it's my risk, isn't it? I'm offering you five thousand dollars now – this minute – for that mine, together with a few acres of the land immediately surrounding it, where it adjoins my holdings. You can spare it, and still have the main part of your pastures. That'll give me a chance to extend the present diggings, see? If I've just bought a hole in the rocks that's my worry. If on the other hand I should find gold that'll be your hard luck. I'm prepared to gamble on it: what do you say?'

'Durned if I know! Feel as though I'm gyppin' yuh...'

Farraday glanced at Sally questioningly and she nodded her blonde head.

'Okay,' Farraday said. 'I reckon I'd be a fool to turn down an offer like that. Jus' the same, Boyd, I think you're crazy!'

'Ever heard of a friend in need?' Wilcot asked; then with a smile he sat down at the table and pulled out his cheque book. After a moment or two he handed the cheque over to the girl. 'Easier for you to hold it,' he smiled.

'It's mighty decent of yuh,' Farraday said. 'Don't think I can't see you're makin' me a gift.'

'I'll see Kyle Endicott when I get back to town,' Wilcot said, mentioning his lawyer. 'He'll fix up the deed of transfer and bring it here for you to sign… Well, I feel better for that! Now I'd better be on my way – and you look after yourself, Henry! 'Bye for now.'

Ken saw him off the ranch and then returned thoughtfully into the room.

'Mighty generous gesture, that!' Farraday declared.

'Yeah,' Ken agreed, rather drily. 'Nice to have a pardner who'll dish out five thousand dollars for a useless mine and a few acres of scorched land when you fall on hard times!'

'Meanin'?'

'Meanin' *is* the mine as dead as it looks? Mebbe you're the one being gypped!'

'Not I! But I'm a businessman an' I may as well have five thousand dollars extra as not. Anyway, the assayer's final report on that mine ten years ago was that it'd been sucked completely dry of any gold.'

'Hmm. Whereabouts is it, exactly? I'd rather like to take a look at it before it ceases to be your property.'

'It ceased to be my property when this cheque was handed over,' Farraday responded, grinning – but Ken shook his head.

'Not quite, Mr Farraday. Let's look at it legally. The mine and surrounding land is still yours while no legal transfer has been signed and the cheque isn't cashed. Anyway, a look-see over the mine can't do any harm, an' I'm pretty sure Wilcot's too nice a guy to raise objections if he caught me doin' it.'

'It's rather an awkward place to get at,' Sally remarked. 'In fact I'd have to show you personally. I'd be glad to do it, if you like?'

'Can't think of anythin' I'd like better,' Ken grinned. Sally nodded, then seemed to bethink herself.

'We'll need torches if we're to look inside the mine...'

'Simple,' Ken said, glancing at Bill. 'Get some oil-torches, Bill, and meet us outside.'

Within a few minutes all three of them were speeding down the trail from Waterfall Valley, kicking up dust into the hot sunshine. The girl rode fast and well, Ken noted. He realized – for perhaps the first time – what an attractive girl she was, the grey riding-trousers and silk shirt revealing her figure to perfection, and the warm breeze sweeping back her blonde hair. There was no doubt that she was an absolute part of the West with just the right touch of steel in her slim wrists to keep control over the fast mare she was riding.

At length she branched off suddenly from the trail to go over tufted scrubland and for a while led the way over short grass until through the fairly thick trees there loomed the foothills of the mountain range. By detours through off-trail ways and amidst rocks they came finally to a broken down area of rotting pit-props and deserted workers' shacks.

'This is it,' the girl said, drawing rein and waving her arm. 'Would you pay five thousand dollars for it? *I* wouldn't.'

Ken dismounted and surveyed the expanse of old mine through sun-dazzled eyes. Then taking one of the oiled wood torches he had brought with him he went forward slowly, leaving the girl in charge of Bill.

After a while he came to cracked boarding which led into the half-planked tunnel-opening marking the mine's entrance. Most of the planks had split away under the heat of the sun, revealing a black void beyond.

Ken peered into it, lighted the torch, then with a wave of his hand to the distant pair he stepped through the jagged opening and into the abysmal gloom of grey rock tunnel beyond. Within seconds he was out of sight of the daylight, following a track where rusted bogey-truck rails still lay. His footsteps echoed hollowly in the cavernous space.

So finally he came to the mineshaft proper. There was no elevator any more – only broken cables where it had been, and a dark hole that went down into the bowels of the mine. Ken studied the roughly constructed timber barrier, decided it was so rotten that an extra good shove might smash in the whole issue; then he picked up a stone and dropped it down the shaft. After some time it re-echoed from stone somewhere far below. Evidently the deserted workings were not flooded.

For a second or two Ken hesitated, then – making up his mind – he threw one leg over the edge of the timber barrier and fished below with his foot for the nearest iron footrest. There was one all right, and one below that again. He began to go down slowly, holding the smoky torch carefully in one hand.

Out in the blazing sunlight Bill and Sally waited for him for almost an hour, sprawled with their backs against a rock and exchanging small talk while the horses nibbled at grass-roots. Sally was intrigued that Bill spent most of the time talking about Emily Bradmore. Then at last Ken came back, filthy dirty, a curious grimness in his lean face.

'Find anythin', boss?' Bill enquired eagerly, helping the girl up.

'Yes – but I've got to check up on it in the town. It's vitally important I go there first. Bill, I want you to see Miss Farraday back to the spread: it isn't safe for her in North Wind. Then join me there quick as you can.'

'Does this mean,' Sally asked, musing, 'that Boyd Wilcot is trying to gyp my dad?'

'Offhand I dunno,' Ken said, still with that curious grimness in his face. 'I'm going to make it my business to find out. In the meantime tell your pop to lay off signing any deed of transfer until he hears from me. Tell him to make some excuse to the lawyer to delay the signing.'

The girl was about to question him further, but Ken didn't give her the chance. Instead he took her arm and helped her back on to her mare. He nodded briefly to Bill and turned towards his horse. Vaulting into the saddle he swung the animal in the direction of North Wind Gap.

'Get goin', Bill. I'll see you later in town.'

Sally and Bill exchanged puzzled glances as Ken disappeared in a cloud of dust, heading at a spanking pace for the town.

'Better do as the boss says,' Bill said. 'I've

an idea that will help your pop with the lawyer.'

Together they headed back to the Straight H, puzzling as to what Ken had discovered in the mine. A hidden goldseam, perhaps?

4

Ken arrived in North Wind Gap smothered in the dust of the trail, just as the noonday sun was blazing relentlessly on the little town.

He watered his horse and then dropped in at Hank's Hash Bar, for a bite to eat. As he ate his face showed that he was doing plenty of thinking meanwhile, and his expression became harsher as he did it. So profound was his concentration that he didn't realize how much time had elapsed. In the end he pushed his cold coffee-cup aside and nodded to himself.

Yeah, I reckon that's somethin' like it, he decided. He glanced up absently through the window, and gave himself a shock. There in the high street, horses neck-reined, were Bill and Sally. Sally! Ken thrust money on the table, grabbed his hat and raced outside.

'Hey, Miss Farraday!' he shouted. 'You gone completely loco?'

Bill and the girl turned at his voice, brought their horses trotting over to where Ken stood frowning by the boardwalk rail.

'What are you doing here?' he demanded, looking at the girl grimly. 'Don't you know you're askin' for a bullet in that pretty head of yourn?'

'I'm not scared of bullets while you're about,' she answered smiling. 'Don't forget I've a debt to pay too for the way I was man-handled. I just couldn't sit back at the ranch listening to Dad raving over his broken arm, and asking questions about the mine I couldn't answer. So I came back with Bill.'

'That's right, boss,' Bill muttered uncomfortably, as Ken's icy grey eyes fixed on him. 'By the way, I gave Sally's father the name of your lawyer in Clover City. Mr Farraday'll tell Wilcot's man that he needs time to consult him.'

'At least you got somethin' right,' Ken growled. 'Now listen up: We're all goin' out of this town right now, and you two are stopping there. I'm taking no chances on Shorty Cartwright or one of his triggermen seeing you and putting lead through you.

We'll lie low somewhere near the burned-out ranch until nightfall, when I've business back in the town.'

'What business, boss?' Bill asked, puzzled. 'Can't you tell us what's a-goin' on?'

'My business is with Shorty Cartwright,' Ken said. 'That's why I can't do much until nightfall. The best time for a word with him is at night, when he'll be in the Blue Dollar. When I've finished there I'll ride out and I'll find you later. Come on – let's get out of here before we're seen!'

As they reached the outskirts of the town unmolested Ken began to breathe a little more freely.

At length they reached a cluster of trees.

'This spot'll do to make camp,' Ken said. 'Be shade from the sun and keep us out of sight of any wandering cowpunchers.' As they sprawled in the grass with their water canteens, Sally began to bombard Ken with questions.

'Why did you have us tell Dad to delay signing? Is it because Wilcot is trying to gyp us?'

'Mebbe...' Ken lighted a cigarette and reflected. 'I don't reckon it's safe to dash at too many ideas, Miss Farra – Durn it!' he burst out, 'I've got to call you Sally! I ain't the sort of fella who can keep formal.'

'I don't like it either, Ken,' the girl smiled.

He nodded in relief. 'That's a help, believe me. Look here, how's about you and me goin' for a walk? Still some time on our hands and it's time we got properly acquainted.'

'I'll stay here and keep a look out along the trails,' Bill said, smiling broadly. 'Just in case anyone might see you,' he added drily.

Sally nodded, and he helped her to her feet. Side by side they strolled across the rough grass in the hot sunshine, the ruins of the Double G away to their right. The girl avoided looking at it as much as possible.

'Y'know,' Ken said presently, throwing away his cigarette, 'I don't reckon to be a detective, Sally, yet I find myself putting two an' two together just like that! I've got a feeling that afore sun-up tomorrow your pop'll be cleared of the charge against him and North Wind'll be a safe place for you and him to come back to.'

The girl's grey eyes turned to him quickly. 'Why do you say that, Ken? Can't you give me some sort of clue?'

He grinned. 'I reckon not. I'm a cautious sort of guy. You'll find out soon enough – granting I can dodge the bullets that may come my way after sundown!'

'Bullets?' Sally looked at him worriedly. 'Promise me you'll take care, Ken.' Then she held out her arms...

At the Straight H, old man Farraday was chafing with baffled impatience. He had obeyed Ken's instructions to the letter, after they had been impressed upon him by Sally and Bill. Not long after Sally and Bill had departed to rejoin Ken in North Wind Gap, Lawyer Kyle Endicott had duly arrived, bringing with him an official deed of transfer for signature. But Farraday had prevaricated over the signing of the deed, claiming that he needed time to study it, and seek his own legal advice. Since he was still unfit to travel, he had to wait for his lawyer to come to see him – and that could not be done until tomorrow morning. Bill had given him the name of Mark Denning, a lawyer in Glover City.

The surprised Endicott had no choice other than to accept the situation. He left the document with Farraday and rode off, promising to return the next day. Endicott was puzzled and disappointed, but certainly not suspicious. Denning was well known to him. He decided not to inform Wilcot of the delay, considering that it might reflect adversely on his own professional competence. No need for Wilcot to know, since he was still convinced that Farraday would sign the document the next day. He knew that Denning would find nothing amiss with it.

After Endicott had left, Farraday studied the deed. It appeared to be perfectly straightforward, and quite in order. The carefully drawn map attached showed the mine, and took in a few acres of surrounding land. On the face of it, it seemed crazy to turn down Wilcot's money, which was sorely needed if he was to rebuild his ranch. Why then had Ken told him not to accept it?

Farraday could only think of one explanation, and the idea swiftly took hold in his mind. Ken had actually been down the mine and inspected it, so obviously he must have *found* something down there. It must have been *gold!* Perhaps the mine was *not* played out, after all... Maybe there had been a rockfall or landslip – not uncommon in old underground mine-workings – which had revealed a new seam of the precious yellow metal? Yes, that had to be it!

Abruptly he made up his mind: he would

ride out to the mine and take a look for himself.

Killing time until after sunset was the hardest job ever for Ken, Sally and Bill, and there was no point in going back and forth to the Straight H in the interval. But at last the brassy orb did disappear behind the horizon and purple night rolled in over the prairie land, signalling the lights to go up in the stores and over the false fronts of North Wind Gap.

Once this happened the three jogged their horses to the main street, then leaving Bill and the girl in shadow cover, Ken continued the journey as far as the Blue Dollar. He tied his horse to the rail and strode through the batwings into the tobacco-fogged interior. Some of the cowpunchers glanced towards him idly, then went on talking. Ken surveyed everything as he ordered whiskey. At last he saw Shorty Cartwright playing cards at a distant table, near the faded blonde and the hanging tub of flowers. Ken smiled to himself, tossed off his drink, then crossed the saloon with easy strides. Reaching Shorty he leaned over his shoulder.

'Got a minute for a few words, Shorty?' he murmured.

Shorty glanced up, jaw tight, eyes bitter. 'Ain't you got no more goddamned sense than to horn in on a card game?' he demanded. 'Git to hell outa here!'

Ken straightened up, hard lights in his grey eyes. He considered the four players for a moment – then all of a sudden he kicked up his right foot under the table and sent it flying. Three of the men toppled backwards in their chairs, cards, chips and drinks spraying all over them.

'You stinkin' coyote–!' Shorty bellowed, his hand blurring down towards his holster – but before he could touch it strong hands twined in his kerchief and at the seat of his pants.

Cursing and struggling he was bundled across the saloon, followed by the belly-laughs of the men who seemed delighted at seeing him at a disadvantage for once.

The contrast between Ken's six-feet plus and the squat Shorty was not without its comical aspect. Nor did Ken let up. He hurled Shorty through the swing-doors and down the steps into the dusty street.

Immediately Shorty whipped out his gun, only to howl with anguish as Ken's hand went down and up. His Colt was smoking and the sixgun had spun out of Shorty's numbed grip.

'Get up!' Ken ordered briefly, coming slowly down the steps. 'Get up, you dirty hyena, before I blast the dirt from under yuh!'

Shorty got up, nursing his tingling fingers. 'What in hell d'yuh want anyway?' he demanded.

'You'll find out. Start walkin' – down the street.' With a Colt muzzle pressed in his back Shorty could do little else. He marched on until forced into a side-alley away from the high-street lamps.

'Turn around,' Ken ordered, and holstered his gun. Then he went on: 'You've got no gun and I've holstered mine. I want some information out of you, even if I have to beat the hide off you to get it!'

Shorty did not even ask what information was required of him. Instead he lunged forward, fists bunched, but an uppercut like a steam-hammer took him on the jaw and plunged him face down in the dust. He shook his spinning head and tasted the salt of blood in his mouth.

'All I want from you,' Ken said, standing over him, 'is the name of the man who told you to run Farraday and his daughter outa town. You ain't got the brains to think that up all by yourself! Come on, speak!'

He hauled Shorty to his feet and then delivered a lefthander that rocked the cowpuncher viciously.

'OK. OK, I'll tell yuh,' Shorty cried, as he saw the muscular arm retract for another blow. 'There ain't no call fer me to take a beatin' over it, I reckon. It was–'

A revolver exploded somewhere down the alleyway. Shorty twirled half round and then crashed on his back and lay still. Ken stared down the alley with narrowed eyes, taken aback by the suddenness of it for a moment – then he streaked towards the spot from which the shot had come. The assassin had vanished round the backs of the ramshackle buildings. Slowly Ken returned to where Shorty was lying and felt his pulse. It had stopped.

For a moment or two Ken reflected, then tugging out his jackknife he snapped open the blade and began to dig ruthlessly for the bullet embedded below Shorty's heart. Once he had it out he dropped it in his pocket and then dragged the dead man into the shadows of the buildings and left him there.

A few seconds later Ken was striding up the street again. He stopped at the Blue

Dollar and entered, his gaze encompassing the assembly for the second time within the hour. As near as he could tell most of the men and the faded blonde singer were in the same positions as earlier – but there were two additions ... Clem Billings and Boyd Wilcot were standing beside the bar, talking, half-emptied whiskey-glasses before them.

Ken relaxed a trifle and strolled forward, ordered a whiskey.

'Hello there!' Wilcot greeted him, turning. 'I believe you just gave Shorty the run out? The boys have been talking about it. I wish I'd been here in time to see it...'

Ken looked beyond him to Clem. 'You see it, Clem?' he asked briefly.

'Nope – but I'd have liked to. I've been in my office until a few moments ago.'

Ken took his drink and swallowed it, set the glass down emphatically on the counter. His next question was somewhat surprising.

'You anything of a gambler, Mr Wilcot?'

'I might be...' Wilcot's dark eyes gave nothing away. 'Why?'

'I reckon that you are. You wear a gambler's string tie. If you're not one now I'm willing to wager you were once.'

'Yes, I gamble – now and again,' Wilcot

admitted. 'Sometimes the stakes are pretty high too. Does it interest you?'

'I think so,' Ken said. 'I'd like to make a gamble with you for that mine you've bought from old man Farraday – that is if you don't mind me mentionin' the deal out loud before Clem here?'

'Not at all,' Wilcot responded; shrugging then to Clem he added, 'I've bought Grey Face Mine and some surrounding land from Farraday. Sort of help him a bit with his finances.'

Clem studied his whiskey-glass and said nothing, but there was a half-formed wondering expression on his face.

'Well?' Wilcot asked. 'What about this gamble, Mr Bradmore?'

'I'd like that mine for myself.' Ken said deliberately. 'I'm suggestin' a sportin' proposition – not cards, for I'm no shakes with those – but shootin'. You see that tub of flowers over there hanging over that blonde?'

Wilcot looked across at it suspended from its three cords and nodded.

'There's a quarter-inch-wide knot-hole in it, facin' us,' Ken went on. 'My wager is this: we both shoot at that tub, one after the other, and whoever blows the knot-hole out wins... That ain't so easy as it looks, neither. It's a small target and a good distance. What say?'

Wilcot chuckled. 'I think you're crazy, Bradmore. Good God, man, I've never used any guns but these in my holsters and I could shoot a gnat at five miles with 'em. You'll stand no chance!'

Ken rested his hands on his Colts. 'I'm willin' to try it, Wilcot, if you are. If you win I'll turn over to you cattle and land to the value of ten thousand dollars, which I can just about scrape up. If I win you transfer that mine to me the moment old man Farraday has signed it to you. Agreed?'

'Surely,' Wilcot said, amused. 'Actually, the deed will have been signed by now. And the boys here and Clem are witnesses to the deal. Right! Who shoots first?'

'You can,' Ken said. 'Clem can be starter. When he gets up to three you fire.'

Clem nodded and Wilcot drew one of his six-shooters from the right holster and levelled it. Clem began counting...

'One...'

Ken eased both his Colts into his hands and cast a hasty look about him. In his mind he photographed the position of the hanging tub of flowers and the two big lamps swinging in the ceiling, and the distance to the batwings...

'Two,' said Clem impassively. 'Three!'

Wilcot fired – clean and straight. The faded blonde jumped dizzily as the tub near her head swayed from the impact of the bullet. The knot-hole had gone, neatly drilled!

'Sort of saved you the trouble, eh?' Wilcot grinned, turning.

Ken didn't answer. Instead both his guns flashed up and fired simultaneously. The twin lights went out in a shattering of glass and plunged the panic-stricken saloon into darkness.

Everything clear in his mind's eye, Ken dived into a scum of swirling men, ploughed through the mass of overturning tables and chairs, and within seconds reached that swinging tub of flowers. With one yank he had it down, clutched it to him, then battered his way through the surging, yelling men to the batwings. Panting hard he stumbled through them and out into the street.

Within seconds he had his horse untied, leaped into the saddle, and headed out of town at the devil's own pace. Behind him voices shouted, revolvers exploded.

He had got beyond the town limit when Bill and the girl caught up with him riding hard.

'What's that you got, boss?' Bill demanded in astonishment, catching sight of the flower-tub in the moonlight. Ken didn't answer. Instead:

'Go back to Sheriff Garson's office,' he ordered, spurring his horse to even greater speed. 'You'll have to detour to avoid the mob that'll be following me after they find Shorty Cartwright. Get hold of Garson and bring him with you to Grey Face Mine as fast as horseflesh can bring him.'

Bill asked no more questions. Veering off he rode hell for leather into the moonlight.

'What's happened? What did you mean about Cartwright?' Sally panted, flogging her own mount to keep pace. 'Can't you tell me?'

'Later,' Ken snapped. 'Only thing I wish right now is that you were tucked away somewheres nice and peaceful. You're plumb scarin' the hide off me when I think of what's followin'!'

More he refused to say and they continued riding hard and fast under the stars and moon until at length they reached the mine. Ken dismounted swiftly, helped the girl down as she insisted on staying beside him, then she hurried with him to the mine's broken-boarding entrance. He spent a moment or two lighting a torch he had brought from his saddle pack, then together they stumbled into the long tunnel leading to the mine's depths.

'We're goin' below,' Ken said grimly. 'You'd better come with me; it'll be safer – though I don't quite figure why nobody's caught up with us yet. OK – over you go.'

He helped her down to the first of the iron footrests and she took the torch from him. He followed her, holding the small tub of flowers tightly to him with one hand. After descending steadily they came to a stony passageway. Ken led the way along it until they found their way blocked by a pile of crumbled rocks. Obviously there had been a big and fairly recent caving in of rock.

'*Is* there gold down here, Ken?' the girl asked excitedly. 'A hidden seam revealed by this cave-in?'

'Not that I could see, but there was – *this!*' Ken's voice was suddenly quieter as he pointed to a spot a few feet away.

Sally looked, then stared hard in the torchlight. The figure of a man was sprawled there, dressed in black riding-trousers and coat. His arms were outflung, his teeth clenched in death. In the middle of his white shirt-front was a rough, bloodstained hole.

'*Jack Andrews!*' Sally whispered, hand to her mouth. 'But – but how did he get here?'

'I reckon he was carried here. Can you think of a better place to hide a dead body than in a mine that hasn't been used for ten years? Did you ever stop to think how hard it is to hide a dead body and be sure no wanderin' cowpuncher will come across it?'

'But, Ken, I don't understand how...'

'Hey there!' bawled a voice from the top of the shaft. 'You down there, Bradmore? Your foreman led me up here...'

'Come right down, Sheriff!' Ken called back. Then there came the sound of Garson's heavy boots scraping on the iron rests, followed by those of Bill Winslow.

'Now, what's this?' Garson demanded, coming to the level and into the torchlight. 'Your foreman tells me– Oh, howdy, Miss Sally! I reckon I never expected to see *you* and – Jack Andrews!' he yelled, catching sight of the sprawled body.

'And here's the bullet I dug out of him earlier today,' Ken said quietly, handing one over from his pocket. 'That's why the wound is so jagged. Bullets make mighty good evidence, and I had the good sense to realize it.'

'Just what's goin' on here?' Garson asked slowly.

'And here,' Ken added, fishing in his shirt pocket, 'is the bullet I dug out of Shorty Cartwright when he was shot dead tonight while I was – er – talkin' to him. I'll explain to you later how he was killed.'

Garson took one bullet in each palm and looked at them. His eyes narrowed suspiciously in the torchlight.

'Better come clean with the rest, Bradmore,' he said bluntly. 'This smells like bad business to me.'

'Last of all...' Ken reached out to the flower-tub and dug his hands in the soil. 'Here is bullet number three...' He pulled it out and examined it, then handed it over. 'Just the same,' he said, 'you'll find, Sheriff, that if you have these three bullets examined by experts, that they have all been fired from the same six-shooter. There's an imperfection in the barrel that leaves a small groove down each bullet as it flies from the muzzle. You can see it faintly. Notice?'

Garson squinted closely at each bullet and his eyes widened. 'Yeah, that's right! But who in blazes...'

'Boyd Wilcot. He fired into this flower-tub tonight – at my request – an' unwittingly condemned himself. He also said out loud before everybody in the Blue Dollar that he'd never used any other guns! Since he used his righthand gun I take it that that's the one he normally uses unless two are called for.'

'Boyd Wilcot! Jumpin' snakes, you mean that he –'

'I mean that he shot Jack Andrews; that he musta sneaked up on Shorty and me when we were talking and closed Shorty's trap before he could say too much. Then he went back to the Blue Dollar and reckoned that he'd only just gotten there.'

'Well, I reckon this evidence is pretty straight,' Garson admitted. 'But why did Wilcot do it?'

'I can only make assumptions,' Ken answered, thinking. 'But I suspected he had somethin' to do with it when he got off so lightly while Farraday and Sally here got the whole works. It just didn't sound natural. It set me wondering if he'd started the rumours against Farraday and mebbe bought off Shorty heavily with dough to pull the run-out. Obviously he had, and at some prearranged signal the fun started. It also struck me after a talk with Clem Billings that only a cattleman could benefit from the set up. What cattleman was left? Only *Wilcot!*'

'That still ain't the reason for Wilcot bumpin' off Andrews,' Garson muttered, scratching his chin.

'I can make a guess at one,' Ken answered. 'Maybe that talk of Wilcot's about being so wealthy isn't true. He admitted only tonight that he gambles sometimes for high stakes, and his whole general air – even his clothes – is that of a gambler; so mebbe he's near broke and needs to be without opposition in his cattle trade. I figure he watched his chance for shootin' Jack Andrews, chose a night when it would look as if Farraday had done it an' then hid the body here...'

'I can't figger him bein' broke, boss, when he offered five thousand dollars for this mine,' Bill muttered, pondering.

'He could raise that amount selling off his assets...' Ken said, breaking off as a sudden voice floated down from above.

'You seem to be getting a bit off-trail down there,' remarked a leisurely voice from the top of the shaft.

'Wilcot!' Ken breathed, starting.

'Maybe I can set you straight on one or two things,' Wilcot proceeded. 'You're fairly close to the truth in a few things, Mr Bradmore, but not quite close enough. I shot Jack Andrews because I owed him a lot of money. I gambled away my fortune two years ago and have fought a losing battle against competition ever since. I decided to get rid of Andrews and frame Farraday to take the blame for it...'

Wilcot paused as though considering his words.

'I had originally planned a genuine necktie party for Farraday and I paid Shorty plenty of dough to do the job – but then there was an unexpected development. It meant that Farraday had got to stay alive so I could legally buy land from him. The only compromise I could make was to hide Andrews' body, and have Farraday and his daughter run out of town on suspicion of having killed him – but Shorty carried it too far. He burned down the ranch and gave Farraday a rough ride that might have killed him. When I protested Shorty merely thought it was part of my act...'

'That's right, he *did* protest!' Sally murmured. 'No wonder!'

'So,' Wilcot resumed, 'after I shot Andrews

I brought his body down here. I thought it would be safe from discovery, after I'd buried it under a pile of rocks...'

'You didn't figger on a landslip, Wilcot!' Ken called up the shaft. 'It dislodged some of the rocks, and when I came down here earlier I saw Andrews' hand showing. I didn't know who it was until I'd pulled the whole body clear.'

'So that's how you got on to me...' Wilcot mused. 'A great pity!' He smiled grimly. 'A pity for you, that is! Now you'll all have to die...'

'Don't be a fool, man! You can't get away with this,' Ken shouted. 'The people from the town must be looking for me: they'll be here any minute...'

'No they won't. I told them I'd overheard you tell your companions that you were headed for Glover City. They're chasing off there now. I rode with them for a while, then pretended my horse was lame, and dropped back. Then I came here, where I was fairly sure you'd really be...'

'What the hell did you mean just now?' Ken asked. 'What was this "unexpected development?" Have you discovered gold in this mine, or–'

'My reasons are none of your business,

Bradmore. Suffice it to say I needed to keep Farraday alive. I was worried a good deal until I found out where Farraday was, and that he was safe – then things seemed to be all right ... until you poked your damned nose in, Bradmore.'

'Tell me somethin', Wilcot,' Sheriff Garson shouted. 'How did Shorty Cartwright get mixed up in this?'

'Shorty had to obey me because I knew a thing or two about his part in that Overland Stage holdup some years ago. Trouble was, he was too thorough. Naturally it was I who shot him tonight before he could say too much.'

'Suppose, through Shorty's thoroughness, Farraday had died?' Garson snapped. 'What then?'

'I'd have figured something out – but it would have been difficult. He didn't, and so things worked out right.'

'Don't be too sure of that, you brute!' Sally stepped forward and addressed Wilcot, looking up the shaft. 'I told Dad to send your lawyer packing! You'll find that he *hasn't* signed your precious deed!'

'Then I'll soon make that old fool change his mind,' Wilcot retorted, though it was apparent that he had been rattled by the girl's words. 'Well, you've had your free confession – or as much as I've chosen to tell you – but if you think you can make use of it you're stark crazy! I've let you people go down there so I can be rid of you and run North Wind Gap the way I want it – which I can once I have Farraday's signature on that deed. It'll bring me unlimited wealth with which I can buy all the support I need.'

Handing the flaming torch to Bill, Ken moved forward cautiously and gripped the lowest shaft footrest, just as a massive chunk of boarding sailed down past him and crashed to the stone floor.

'He's trying to kick the shaft top in!' Sally cried hoarsely. 'To bury us!'

Ken went upwards doggedly. Time and again chunks of stone hit his shoulders and numbed him, nearly dislodging him from his hold – but the mass of wood and stone that would have sealed up the shaft was evidently tougher than it looked – for all Wilcot's kickings and thumpings failed to entirely dislodge it.

Slowly Ken went higher, then as he heard the sounds of the ascent, Wilcot broke off his efforts and peered over the edge. His gun blazed thunderously and a bullet from his snap shot whanged the stone wall, missing Ken only by inches. Wilcot sighted for a second shot… Whisking out his right-hand gun Bill Winslow fired back from below, causing Wilcot to retreat from the edge of the shaft. It enabled Ken to reach the top, and he heard the sound of stumbling, running feet in loose stones. He started swiftly in pursuit.

In the darkness, Ken realized that shooting was hopeless, though Wilcot risked it now and again and unwittingly revealed his position thereby. Ken fired back, missed, and chased onwards towards the half-boarded tunnel entrance. He wasn't quick enough to stop Wilcot vaulting to his horse. Wilcot swung the dun round in the bright moonlight and spurred him forward to breakneck speed.

Ken fired again, futilely, then dived for his own horse, plumped in the saddle, and hurtled forward. At a thunderous pace he raced out of the rocky little depression and across the bare moonlit scrub, following the balloon of dust from the fleeing Wilcot. Now and again a bullet zipped dangerously close.

5

Henry Farraday was not a happy man. After slowly cantering out of the Straight H, taking care that no one saw him leave – in case they tried to stop him – he had quickly discovered that riding a horse with only one arm was fraught with danger. His broken left arm, set in splints, and tightly bound up in a sling, was useless. Riding at any speed using only his right hand to grip the reins would only serve to pitch him right out of the saddle and break his neck. He must have been crazy to set out on this journey to the mine.

But Farraday was nothing if not stubborn: he had to know the truth about the mine. And so he continued on his way, albeit travelling at an agonizingly slow pace. Fortunately, he'd had the sense to pack a water-bottle and some provisions for himself and his horse in his saddlebag. Hours passed; the late afternoon turned into evening, and then into night. He took a blanket from his saddlebag and draped it awkwardly around his shoulders to keep out the increasing chill. He had to keep going, and when he reached the mine entrance, he could bed down for the night, using his saddle as a pillow, and then await the daylight...

Suddenly Farraday alerted as he heard the sounds of gunfire some distance ahead of him. It seemed to be coming from the direction of the mine! He peered desperately ahead of him, trying to pierce the night gloom. Suddenly the sound of galloping hoofs, punctuated by further shots, sounded dangerously close. He caught sight of the brief flame of a Colt, then a large grey blur loomed up. His horse whinnied and shied up on its hind legs, and Farraday clutched desperately at the reins with his one good arm.

Wilcot had turned in the saddle to loose off a snap shot at his pursuer. He did not see Farraday and his horse loom out of the murk directly ahead of him until it was too late. There was a sickening thud of horse-flesh, the frenzied neighing and snorting of the terrified entangled animals, and suddenly both men were flung from their saddles. A hoarse cry jerked from Wilcot's lips as his horse went sprawling and he spun head over heels in the dust, his gun flying away from him, and the breath completely knocked from his bruised body. Dazed, he lay breathing hard, unable at first to comprehend what had happened to him.

The pounding of hoofs as Ken drew level pierced the fog of pain and brought comprehension of his perilous position. He squirmed on to his knees, striving to pull his remaining gun free of its holster. He got it out and straightened to his feet just as Ken vaulted from the saddle and hurtled towards him. As the gun trigger cocked, a smashing blow in the middle doubled him up in anguish – then he was forced to straighten again before an uppercut that nearly guillotined his tongue between his teeth.

Again Ken struck, and again, driving the blows with all the power of his steel-strong arms. Wilcot instinctively fought back, and somehow landed a left with a sting in it to Ken's face. Incensed, Ken lashed back a right that lifted Wilcot off his feet. Wilcot crumpled back into the dust and lay groaning. Stepping forward, Ken brought the barrel of his gun sharply across Wilcot's head. His groaning ceased abruptly as he crashed into complete unconsciousness. The silence that followed was punctuated by a faint groan from nearby.

Ken swung round and caught sight of a dark, twisted shape lying perhaps ten yards away. He ran across to it, dropped to his knees in the dust. It was the body of a man! But who could...?

A gasp escaped Ken as he suddenly recognized the contorted features of Henry Farraday in the bright moonlight.

'Mr Farraday! It's me – Ken! Are you...'

'Ken?' Farraday's voice was a sepulchral whisper, a death rattle. 'I'm finished, son... Back's broken... *Sally!* My little gal... Look... after her! *Promise me...*' Farraday gave a choking cough as his mouth filled with blood. His eyes glazed and his head jerked to one side. He lay unmoving in Ken's arms.

'I promise, old-timer,' Ken whispered, getting to his feet as the sound of more drumming hoofs sounded behind him.

It was the sheriff, Sally, and Bill Winslow, who drew rein in the moonlight.

'Wilcot's all yours, Sheriff,' Ken said dully, wiping his sleeve over his face and his suddenly misted eyes. 'That's him lying over there where I slugged him.' He pointed to the sprawled body nearby.

'Look around for his guns – they'll be on

the ground somewhere: one of them is the piece of evidence you'll need for the bullets.'

Garson jumped down from his horse with alacrity, went over and snapped handcuffs over the unconscious Wilcot's wrists.

'Who – who is that other man, Ken?' Sally's voice sounded through the gloom as she dismounted and came hurrying forward. 'Does he need help? I...'

Ken caught her slim figure and stopped her going forward. 'He's beyond help, I'm afraid. He's...' He hesitated, unable to speak for the moment.

Bill Winslow meanwhile was striding forward and dropped to his knees beside the still figure. Gingerly, he turned him over from where he lay on his side.

'*Old man Farraday!*' he gasped involuntarily. 'He's dead! Oh, my God! My God...'

Behind him Sally gave a little scream and crumpled into Ken's arms.

The following weeks were something of a blur for Sally Farraday. The death of her father had come as a tremendous blow. She blamed herself. If only she had stayed with him, instead of insisting on riding off with Bill, she might have prevented him setting forth on his fatal journey. For the first few days after his death she had been inconsolable, but gradually she sorted out her emotions, and realized that life had to go on: one could not live with the dead.

Ken Bradmore was a tower of strength and comfort; he made all the arrangements for her father's funeral, and also arranged for his sister to come and stay with her. Whilst Emily Bradmore looked after Sally at the Hillview Hotel in the town, Ken – helped by some of the boys of his Straight H outfit, together with friends of Sheriff Garson – set about rebuilding the burned-out ranch house and corrals.

His own ranch in Waterfall Valley was meanwhile being capably looked after by Bill Winslow; who also managed to fit in numerous visits of his own, both to help Ken and the boys, and also to visit Emily and Sally in the town.

Sheriff Garson took a grim satisfaction in arranging for the trial of his prisoner, Boyd Wilcot. The case was heard in the town schoolroom, specially converted for use as a courthouse, and presided over by a circuit Judge. Sally had been too upset to attend and give evidence, but Ken was the main witness for the prosecution, and his testimony, and the evidence provided by the bullets he had given to Sheriff Garson, was devastating. Boyd Wilcot was found guilty of the murder of Jack Andrews and Shorty Cartwight, and also the involuntary manslaughter of Henry Farraday. He was duly hanged.

There were few – if any – in the town who mourned his passing. The one exception might have been a mysterious woman, who had arrived from out of town two days after the trial. She was the only visitor to Wilcot's condemned cell – other than Kyle Endicott, his lawyer. She kept herself heavily veiled, and afterwards stayed overnight with the lawyer and his wife. The next morning she made a final, private visit to Wilcot's cell, then took an afternoon stagecoach out of town. She did not stay for the execution that was scheduled for the following day. The incident and the woman were soon forgotten.

Then one morning Sally found herself being driven in an ancient buckboard out into the countryside, Emily Bradmore seated alongside her. Their driver, Seth Aitken, a sun-wizened old-timer, ignored Sally's questions as to their destination. Emily, for her part, only smiled broadly as Sally became more and more exasperated.

'Emmy – for goodness sake, tell me where

we're *going...*' Sally broke off, as the buckboard took a distinct turn at a fork in the trail, heading across a great field of golden brittle-brush with the lord's candles nodding in the scented breeze blowing down from the distant Pinga mountains.

'This – this is the trail to the remains of the Double G,' Sally said, with a sideways glance at Emily Bradmore.

'Hardly "remains" Sally – take a look ahead!'

Sally followed the direction of the smiling woman's pointing finger and gave a little start. She found herself gazing at a distant vision of a newly-built ranch house, moderately filled corrals, and a number of punchers going back and forth about their jobs. The new Double G had literally emerged, phoenix-like, from the ashes of the old.

'Your new home,' Emily commented drily. 'Ready and waiting for you to move in.'

Sally flashed her a confused glance.

'It's – it's wonderful! I knew Ken was working on it, but I never realized he'd managed to... Oh, but I *can't* live there!' She broke off in dismay.

'Why ever not?'

'I – I can't possibly run the place on my

own. You and Ken – and Bill too – will be going back to your own ranch, the Straight H...'

Emily smiled, and said nothing.

At length the ranch was reached, and Seth Aitken drove the buckboard through the open gateway and then brought the buckboard to a halt outside the ranch-house veranda. Sally alighted and walked forward. Behind her Emily was paying the driver and giving him further instructions, but Sally did not hear what was being said. She was busy studying the log-walled structure in pleased surprise, her eyes travelling to the screen door, the main window – at which she briefly glimpsed two watching figures – and then the four steps leading up to the porch.

It was not particularly large. The ranch house was rather like a sprawling wooden bungalow of moderate dimensions; there were a few scattered outhouses, a big yard fenced round with wire, and one large corral enclosed by thorny ocotillo bushes, with a firmly secured gate. In this area there moved about seventy steers, blatting uneasily at intervals. Sally realized that Ken must have transferred some of his own herd from the Straight H.

At a sudden sound behind her she turned in surprise, to see the buckboard driving away. Before she could ask questions, the screen door opened, and Ken Bradmore and Bill Winslow emerged. They came down the steps.

Winslow was smiling broadly; Ken less so. He looked a little uncertain of himself.

To Sally's astonishment, Emily threw her arms around Bill and gave him a resounding kiss. Ken quickly stepped forward and took Sally's hand in a gentle grip.

'Hello, Sally. Hope you're not too disappointed?'

'Disappointed? Of course not! I think you've worked wonders, considering that...'

'Let me show you inside,' Ken said, taking her arm.

'Go ahead. Don't mind us!' Emily said, smiling over Bill's shoulder as Sally stood hesitating. 'Bill and I have things to discuss ... about our wedding!' she added drily, holding out her right hand. The ring that Bill had just slipped on to her third finger sparkled in the bright sunlight.

Sally realized with something of a shock that she should not have been as surprised as she was. Bill had been a regular visitor to their hotel, joining them for meals and trips around town. With a guilty start she realized that for much of the past few weeks she had been so wrapped up in her own sorrows that she had not noticed the obvious bond between them.

'Oh, Emily ... Bill – this is wonderful! Please forgive me – I never realized. I'm so happy for you...'

'Thanks, Sally,' Bill smiled. 'We're happy for you, too.'

Before the significance of the remark registered, Ken led her inside.

They stepped through a small hall into a big living-room. The large window admitted plenty of light, but Sally noticed there were brightly burnished oil-lamps on a big wooden table in the centre of the room. Against one wall was a bookcase-bureau, the lower desk portion being open and revealing papers, invoices, and what seemed to be ledgers.

For the rest there were chairs, a sideboard and mirror, and a rocking-chair by the window. The walls of the room were seasoned logs, the chinks stopped with red clay. The floor was also wooden, its bareness relieved by cocoa-matting and, near the large brick fireplace, was a magnificent bearskin rug. Certainly there was nothing reminiscent of an emperor's palace about the place, but Sally's mind was suddenly teeming with ideas as to how it might be improved.

'I know what you're thinking, Sally,' Ken said. 'I know the place badly needs a woman's touch...'

Sally laughed. 'Don't put yourself down, Ken. I think what you've done is just wonderful.'

She turned and began to walk slowly about the room, studying it. She surveyed the walls on which, at intervals, hung crossed rifles and some Indian artefacts. Finally she came to looking at the fireplace. Logs and thin wood were arranged on it.

She was still considering it when Ken came forward and set the mass on fire.

'It gets cold in here later on,' he said cryptically. 'Let me show you the rest of the house.'

He led the way from the room, across the narrow strip of hall, to another door. Sally stepped into a curtained room and again surveyed as the oil-lamp was lit.

The room smelled of newly-aired linen. A large double bed was by the window. Near to it was a dresser, and a wardrobe stood in another corner.

Sally looked again at the double bed and felt her cheeks suffuse with colour. When she turned in confusion, Ken took her into his arms.

A month later, there was a double wedding. Ken gave the Straight H to Emily and Bill as a wedding present, and moved into the Double G with his bride.

He had kept his vow to the dying Henry Farraday.

6

'I keep a-tellin' yuh, ma'am, there jest ain't no sense to this ride o'yourn! Theer *ain't* no Double G spread any more! It wus burned down last night. It's a plain waste of horseflesh drivin' out heer.'

Seth Aitken, driver of the ancient station buckboard, spat casually into the dust at the side of the valley trail and whipped the bony mare into greater activity.

'I'm not doubting your word, Mr Aitken,' the girl beside him responded, her voice taut. 'It's just that – that I've got to see it with my own eyes to believe it.'

'OK, ma'am, have it your own way.' Seth growled. 'Wimmin allus did take a lot of convincin', I reckon.'

Sally Bradmore became silent again. She reflected on how Ken's sister, Emily, would take the news – and her husband and Ken's best friend, Bill Winslow. Sally had spent the past two months at their Straight H ranch, having offered her assistance at the birth of their first child. They had been delivered of a healthy baby boy, but the birth had not been without complications for Emily. So, with Ken's ready agreement, Sally had stayed on with her, helping to look after the baby and nurse Emily back to health.

In this way she had repaid the great debt she herself had owed Emily the previous year, when Emily had stayed with her after her own father's death. Even now, she had not been too happy about leaving them, but Emily and Bill had insisted that they could now manage. And, deep down, she knew that she owed it to Ken to get back to him and help in the re-establishment of the Double G.

Yes, Emily and Bill had plenty on their plate at the moment, she decided. Best not to send word about her own stunning setback ... at least, not until she had talked to

Ken about it. But where *was* Ken?

Behind her, in the wagon, reposed her suitcase. Around her, as far as she could see, as they came at last in the grey foothills of the mountains, were wild verbena and purple hyptis, slashed here and there with the grey, red, orange, and yellow of rock lichens. Unexpectedly, at other points, purple penstemon loomed. Out beyond these fields were the scarlet patchworks of octillo, merged indescribably into the salmon-pink and orange of chollas and opuntias. There seemed to be no end to nature's handiwork wherever the eye chose to rove.

Arizona, at that moment, was in the spring of the year – at its very best indeed, and here nature offered the finest colourings and blooms. Only Sally Bradmore had no eye for them. She was overwhelmed with the one staggering realization that had been hammering into her ever since getting off the stage in North Wind Gap itself.

'I *can't* believe it, Mr Aitken!' she insisted again. 'The Double G was destroyed by arson on the orders of Boyd Wilcot more than a year ago, but Ken had rebuilt it completely! Rebuilt it with his own hands! And Wilcot was hanged, and all his

96

supporters rounded up by Sheriff Garson.'

'Yep, I knows all that, ma'am. I'm mighty sorry ter be the one as broke yuh the news,' Aitken said. 'It sure is a helluva tragedy. But I guess that sometimes history repeats ... like sardines,' he added elliptically.

'There's nobody who could possibly have *done* such a thing! I've been away for two months, helping Ken's sister and her husband over in Waterfall Valley. Right up to yesterday Ken had been writing me every week. Now you say he's gone and that the ranch is burned down!'

'Yeah,' Seth Aitken agreed morosely. 'Reckon that's it.'

'But how could such a thing happen *again?* What about Sheriff Garson? It's his job to keep law and order around here...'

'Sure it is – an' Pat Garson is one of th' best sheriffs we ever had hereabouts. I don't jest know how't figger it, ma'am,' Seth added, squinting into the hot blaze of the afternoon sunlight. 'Last night th' spread were burned down, but nobody saw it 'til it wus destroyed. As fer your husband – I jest don't know *where* he is.'

'Who was the first to see the remains of the fire?' the girl asked sharply.

'A puncher, I think it were – an' he

reported it to th' sheriff. He wus a-ridin' through th' valley here an' saw th' fire as he passed.'

Mystified, stunned indeed, by the incredible thought that her husband had vanished and their property burned down, Sally became quiet again. Beside her, Seth Aitken continued to urge the mare onwards – and presently, bumping in the hardened dirt of the valley trail, the wagon rounded a bend and gave the two passengers a vision of a prosperous ranch house, well-filled corrals, and punchers going back and forth about their jobs. Behind the ranch extended mile upon mile of rich pasture land. This was the Treble Circle, which had formerly belonged to the late Boyd Wilcot.

'Who owns that?' Sally asked. 'It was still empty when I left...' But her voice held no real interest.

'Gal by th' name of Beatrice Alland. Eddicated she is – like yourself, an' be about your age, too. She took over the Treble Circle recent, after lawyer Endicott finally sorted out t'legal side... Reckon she'll make good thing of it: tougher meat than Wilcot were. If your husband's ranch hadn't ha' burned down she'd've bin your nearest neighbour. Her spread, yours, and Clem

Billings' Flying S – you'll remember as how he bought it last year from Jack Andrews' sister after Jack wus shot – at the other end of th' valley, make up th' only three round herebouts. Yourn was in th' middle yonder...'

Seth's arm jerked up and Sally took her grey eyes from the Treble Circle to gaze into the dusty distances where lay a blackened area, the mesquite stumps of the corral fence, charred and broken, being the only things left standing.

Opposite where the double gates should have been Seth drew up the wagon and the girl jumped down into the dust. Slowly, still with that feeling of witnessing something unreal, she advanced into what had been the yard and stood gazing around her.

Nothing but ruin. Corrals empty and ash-covered ranch house destroyed; the dry grass flame-scorched to the roots. As she gradually turned she encompassed the distant vision of Beatrice Alland's Treble Circle in one direction, and Clem Billings' Flying S in the other. And where she was standing there was nothing at all. She found tears starting suddenly in her eyes and blinked them away ashamedly.

'I wus right, wasn't I?' Seth called, from

the wagon-seat. Sally turned and wandered back to him disconsolately.

'Yes,' she muttered. 'You were right. But I can't understand it! Was it accident, design, or what? Where *is* Ken? I've got to find him somehow. Without him I'm just – just sunk! I've only a little money, and I can't go back to Ken's sister as she is right now, and...'

She broke off, the tears she had insisted on fighting suddenly gaining the upper hand.

'Hey, now,' Seth protested, jumping down beside her with concern on his leathery face. 'Take it easy, ma'am. There'll be some sort of explanation some place: you see if there ain't. Bes' thing y'can do is come back with me into town an' put up at the Hillview Hotel. Then y'can figger out what you'll do next.'

Sally nodded half stupidly, her eyes still drowsy. 'You just can't realize what an awful shock this is to me,' she said haltingly.

'I reckon I can,' Seth assured her, helping her up again to the buckboard seat. 'Jest leave it t'me. I'll fix yuh up at th' hotel pronto. Then I reckon yuh'd bes' see th' sheriff. If anybody knows about Ken Bradmore, he oughta.'

Two hours later, after having registered herself at the Hillview, Sally Bradmore was in possession of herself again. From desolate grief her mood had changed to one of grim curiosity and smouldering fury. The destruction of the ranch by fire was baffling enough, but the utter disappearance of her husband, whose last letter had promised that he would be waiting for her at the staging-point when her coach got in that day, was something that had to be explained immediately.

The moment she had bathed and changed from her two-piece into a frock more befitting the torrid afternoon, she left the hotel and explored the ramshackle wooden fronted town of North Wind until she found Sheriff Garson's office.

Bluff and heavily built, he greeted her genially – and in some surprise – as she entered.

'Afternoon, ma'am...' He drew up a chair from beside his desk and motioned the girl to it. 'Good to see you back again. Everythin' OK with Ken's sister?'

'Yes, she has a fine boy, William junior ... but it's *Ken* I came here about, Sheriff! And our ranch being destroyed by fire again! It's ... it's...' Sally was unable to continue for the moment.

'Yeah, I know.' The sheriff settled in his

swivel-chair and the geniality of his face had vanished in grim sympathy. 'I'm real sorry, ma'am. Ken an' I were friends, and—'

'Where *is* Ken?' the girl interrupted, her mouth hard. 'What's been going on, Sheriff? Ken was to have met me at the coach station – and instead I find him gone, the ranch destroyed, and the cattle heaven knows where. That needs explaining, especially from you. As sheriff, you are responsible for law and order in this territory.'

'I'm afraid there's nothin' I can tell you,' Garson replied, sighing. 'I wish there was. Can't get much information becos Ken ran the ranch himself; no boys to help him, who might have had an angle on things. All I can tell you is that last night a puncher came into my place, down the road apiece, to tell me that the Double G was burning. I rode out there, but it was too late to do anythin'. It had burned itself out. I had a posse of men try an' find if any cattle was around, but they came back with the news that they couldn't find anything. As for Ken, I've heard nothin' of him since. Only thing I can think of is that the place caught fire accidental somehow, and Ken just perished in the flames. Happens at times in these arid parts.'

'But surely you've searched the ruins for traces of his body?' Sally demanded.

'I sure did, the moment the ashes was cool. But there aren't no traces. Those sorts of fires are mighty fierce, Mrs Bradmore. They burn a body good, believe you me.'

'But, Sheriff, supposing he'd crawled away from the fire?'

'I thought of that, too. We searched everywhere within three miles without finding a sign of him – an' if he'd escaped unhurt he'd have turned up, wouldn't he? I can only think he died – like I said.'

Sheriff Garson became silent, wishing he had not had to make such statements. His keen dark eyes studied the effect on the girl. Her firm mouth was trembling a little and the look of bewildered horror had come back into her grey eyes.

'I'm almighty sorry, Mrs Bradmore, to have to–'

'You can't help it, Sheriff,' she said, with a wooden kind of smile. 'Thanks for telling me as much as you have...' She got to her feet and stood thinking for a moment; then she said slowly, 'You know, it seems rather odd to me that it had to be a *puncher* who saw the fire. Why wasn't it seen by one or other of the neighbouring ranchers? That

Miss Alland, for instance – or Clem Billings at the Flying S?'

The sheriff reflected. 'Don't rightly know why they didn't see it – 'less they happened to be out. They go places together. Just the way things happened, I s'pose.'

'Yes, I suppose so,' Sally admitted, sighing. 'Well, thanks anyway, Sheriff. If you get any news I'm at the Hillview Hotel across the road.'

'OK – and I'll keep my eyes open,' he promised, shaking hands.

Sally left the office, commencing a slow stroll along the boardwalk as she tried to think things out. She still was not convinced by what she had heard. Not that she doubted the sheriff, but that her husband – young, agile, ambitious – could be so careless as to die in an accidental fire was a conception she just could not accept.

Ignoring the glances from the men and women who passed her, some of whom paused to stare curiously at her, her thoughts moved from the depressing riddle of her husband and the destroyed ranch to herself. How was she going to continue living? What money she had would not last much beyond a month or so, and she had no intention of going back to the Straight H.

Emily and Bill would welcome her with open arms and every sympathy, of course, but it would completely disrupt their own newfound happiness following the birth of their son.

Everything had been banked on a happy future with Ken and the gradual building-up of the cattle-dealing he had handled from the Double G. Now with all that wiped out... She came to a halt, leaning on the rail of the boardwalk and gazing into the dusty street. There was a general stores, a livery stable, an assayer's, lawyer Endicott's office, a drug store, a big rooming-house, a tin tabernacle, and a conglomeration of two-storied dwellings. That was all. If she had to make her life in *this* after remaking the Double G...

She shook her blonde head drearily, left the boardwalk, and crossed the street back to her hotel. Here she had a meal, spent a couple of hours in her room resting and thinking; then as darkness was falling she left the hotel again.

This time, so as not to draw too much attention to herself, or so she hoped, she was attired in a shirt, riding-trousers, and half-boots. At the back of her mind was the resolve to see if some of the habitués of the Blue Dollar saloon could throw some light on the mystery of her husband. In there, with tongues loosened by drink and company, she might discover something. The persistent notion of foul play in the back of her mind just would not be silenced.

Her decision was courageous. She realized just *how* courageous when she passed through the Blue Dollar's batwings just after sunset. The air of the place struck her violently after the fresh sweetness of the wind outside. It stank of liquor and bodies and was clogged with rank tobacco fumes. Amidst the blur loomed punchers, Mexicans, half-breeds, cattle-dealers, and women – some overpainted and underclad; whilst across the confusion there beat incessant noise. It came from voices, a two-piece orchestra on a rickety rostrum, the clink of glasses, and the rattle of poker chips.

Breathing a trifle harder and trying to control her nervousness Sally went forward slowly into the haze, towards the bar. Punchers turned to look at her and then glanced significantly at one another. Women surveyed her in embarrassed sympathy.

'Evening, ma'am,' the stout barkeep greeted as she approached, and as he polished a glass vigorously his eyes strayed to her wealth of blonde hair. 'Sump'n I can git you?'

'Er – yes. I – I'd like a brandy and soda.' She had had one once, she remembered, and survived it.

'B and S – OK!'

It was poured out and handed to her. She paid and then stood playing with her fingers upon the glass. In the back-bar mirrors she surveyed the saloon again. She could not be quite sure but it did look as though the eye of every man in the place was fixed on her, Partly it was her own fault. The silk shirt and riding-pants were extremely revealing.

'You don't want that firewater, kid – try gin,' a voice beside her suggested, and she turned sharply.

A rangy six-footer, his sombrero cuffed up on his forehead, was standing grinning at her, supporting himself with his elbows on the bar counter. He was handsome enough after a fashion, deeply tanned, but there was a look in his eyes from which Sally's feminine instincts immediately recoiled.

'I prefer what I have, thank you,' she told him coldly, and turned away.

'You don't *have* t'be unfriendly, do yuh?' the cowboy enquired, and through the mirrors she saw him wink at his colleagues seated nearby. 'We like t'be sociable with the women who come to our little town – 'specially when they's as purty as you.' He motioned. 'Hey, Jake – a gin for the little lady!'

'I don't want it!' Sally snapped, her cheeks flaming as she glared at him. 'Will you please stop bothering me?'

His only response was to grin all the more. Grabbing her arm he forced her towards him looking down into her frightened face.

'Unsociable gal, ain't you?' he asked drily. 'I reckon, come to think on it, that you must be Ken Bradmore's wife: he were shootin' his face off about you comin' back only the other night. I was a friend of his, so I think that entitles me to a little kiss, doesn't it?'

Sally struggled savagely to tear herself free. Failing in this she kicked his shin violently. He still grinned and caught her other arm, forcing her tightly against his lean, iron-hard body.

'Leave the girl alone, Lefty!' a voice ordered.

'Huh?' The puncher turned in angry surprise and, breathing hard, Sally fell back against the counter, scooping the dishevelled hair from her face.

A powerful, broad-shouldered man in his

late thirties was standing just behind the puncher – a swarthily dark man in a black cutaway coat, grey riding-trousers, and black Stetson.

'Don't know how to keep your hands off a woman, do you?' he demanded, and there was culture in his voice. 'I guess it is about time you were taught...'

Lefty's hands flashed up to protect himself but he was not quick enough. The big fellow's right slammed out in a blinding uppercut. It took Lefty under the jaw and sent him flying backwards across the table at which his comrades were seated. They went down with him in a swamping of beer, glasses, and overturned table.

'An' take it easy,' the big fellow advised, whipping a .38 from his right holster.

Fingering his chin the puncher got up. For a moment he stood glaring, then he relaxed and gave a shrug of indifference.

'OK, if that's the way you want it. Ain't fun knowing a gal if she ain't sociable, anyway.'

'Any more like that from you, you low-down polecat, and I'll skin the hide off you,' the man warned; then he turned and gripped Sally's arm possessively. 'This way,' he instructed, and she was too bewildered to argue.

He steered her through the crowd to a quiet corner table and pulled out a chair for her. He took off his Stetson, sat down opposite her and smiled reassuringly. 'You'll be safe enough here with me,' he told her.

'Thank you,' Sally said. 'It's Mr Billings, isn't it?'

7

'Call me Clem.' Billings smiled. 'After all, since I bought the Flying S, that makes us neighbours.' He reflected, then frowned. 'At least we *were* neighbours until...'

'Until my ranch burned down again,' Sally finished quietly. 'And – and I'd like to thank you for helping me as you did back there.'

'That's OK,' he smiled. 'The boys around here get outa hand now and again when they see a good-looker like you. You're different from the wooden-faced gals who usually flourish around here... Have a drink, to replace the one you didn't get?'

'I'd rather not, thanks. I don't drink really. I'm only in this place at all to try and find out what's happened to my husband.'

Clem Billings studied her for a moment without answering; then he called a waiter over and ordered a beer for himself. When it had arrived he contemplated it and said slowly:

'Afraid I can't help you, Mrs Bradmore, concernin' Ken. All I know is that his spread was burned down last night and he hasn't bin heard of since.'

'That's what everybody says – including the sheriff! But I have the feeling that there's been foul play somewhere.'

'Well, that's possible, of course – in these parts. Things get a bit lawless sometimes. Take the late Boyd Wilcot, for instance...' Catching Sally's expression at the mention of the man who had killed her father, he hastily switched the conversation. 'Just the same, Mrs Bradmore, I was a friend of Ken's, being his neighbour, an' it never struck me that he had any enemies. I'm more inclined to think it was an accident that his place caught fire, and that mebbe he died in it.'

'I don't believe it!' Sally declared flatly. 'Ken wouldn't do a thing like that. He is – or was – too alert. There's more behind it, and I've got to find out what.' Billings took a draught from his glass and put it down again.

'I'd like to help you, Mrs Bradmore. You're not goin' to learn much by coming into a place like this: you'd hogtie yourself with no end of trouble. But since Ken was my neighbour and friend I'll lend a hand. Matter of fact I've wondered myself what really happened, only since it doesn't – or didn't – strictly concern me I made no enquiries. But I will now, to help you. In the meantime...' He looked at her thoughtfully. 'How do you propose to carry on? Got money of your own, I suppose?'

'I can last a little while. Then I'll have to use what remains of our savings. Most of our money went into restocking the Double G.'

'Mmmm – which isn't too good. It may take a while to find out what really happened to Ken.' The big saloon-owner and rancher mused for a while and then lifted his eyes again. 'I've an idea,' he said, 'dependin' on how you like the notion.'

'You've helped me so far,' Sally smiled. 'I'd like to hear it.'

'OK then. You'll have seen the general stores down the street here? Yeah – well, it's mine. I own it along with some other properties. I had a manageress in it till recently, but she quit to go to Glover City to nurse her old man. I could do with a new manageress – an' you look as though you might do.' Then as he saw the girl hesitating Billings added, 'There's nothin' to it, Mrs Bradmore, for an educated woman like yourself. Only a matter of seeing that the two women I have there do their proper jobs. You do the buyin' – and sellin' too when you have the time. It pays around fifteen dollars a week – to you leastways. At least it'll be somethin' to keep you goin'.'

Sally reflected through a long interval, then she gave a slow, uncertain smile.

'It's wonderfully generous of you, Mr. Billings, only I–'

'I know what you're thinkin',' he interrupted. 'Take it from me, Mrs Bradmore, there's no strings attached. Call it a neighbourly act, if you like, till you get yourself straightened out – or till I can perhaps find out what happened to Ken. The West isn't *entirely* filled with bad men, you know,' he added drily. 'I was goin' to look for a manageress, anyhow, but you'll do. If you like the idea you can start tomorrow mornin' and go on livin' where you are now. Is it the hotel or Ma Brayson's roomin' house?'

'I'm at the hotel...' Sally made an end of the small, niggling doubts at the back of her mind, chiefly because this was no time to be choosy. 'I'll take it,' she said. 'And thanks again for your generosity, Mr Billings.'

The following morning Sally took up her new duties in a lighter frame of mind. She had slept well, despite the worries with which she was beset, and due reflection had convinced her that in the position of general store manageress she could accomplish two things – keep herself going financially and at the same time pick up gossip from the customers, get to know them, maybe trace through casual remarks the real facts connected with her husband's mysterious fate.

At the store, Billings, perfectly polite, only stayed long enough to initiate her into what duties there were and introduce her to the two women assistants, both of them bovine and slow-moving. Then he departed to attend to business elsewhere, but not before he had placed at her disposal a bright little pinto and a .38 in case she needed to protect herself against any 'local character' with less morals than sense. Thus equipped she faced her occupation – and spent the first day orientating herself and getting on friendly terms with the two assistants.

On the whole, business was fairly brisk, and she did much of the serving herself since she mainly had women to deal with; but not from any of them did she learn anything worthwhile concerning her husband's fate.

In the three days that followed, Billings looked in from time to time, exchanged a few business comments and remarked that, for all his efforts, he had not learned anything. Slowly the grim thought began to cloud on Sally again that her husband, after all, must have perished in an accidental fire. There seemed to be no other answer. Then on the fourth morning she found herself faced with a different type of customer. For some time he had been prowling around the store as though trying to make up his mind. Now he stood looking at Sally from the other side of the counter.

He was a small-built man in a flannel shirt, shaggy wolfskin coat, patched riding-trousers, and dusty half-boots. A round, coonskin hat was pushed back on his grizzled white hair. His coat was flowing open so that there was just a glimpse of the big .45 swinging loosely on a slack cartridge belt.

'Mornin',' he greeted, and though he sounded fierce the effect was more comical than terrifying.

As he spoke he peered at Sally with intense blue eyes gleaming against a leathery, burned-in brown face.

'Good morning,' Sally responded politely, forcing a smile. 'Is there something I can do for you?'

'Nope; I reckon not. More like sump'n I c'n do fer you.' He glanced about him at the almost deserted store and then leaned confidentially over the counter. 'Yuh don't know me, of course – but most people hereabouts do. I'm Eph Millthorn. They calls me "Tin Pan". Reckon some of th' folks think I'm loco...' He chuckled to himself and revealed a nearly toothless mouth.

'Be dad-blamed if they ain't right in some ways! Bin washin' dirt for twen'y year now an' I ain't had so much as a sniff of a bonanza. But mebbe I will someday.'

It took Sally, not thoroughly versed in the local idiom some seconds to grasp his meaning.

'You mean you're a gold-prospector?' she asked.

'Yep.' He looked at her fiercely. 'That's why they calls me "Tin Pan". I've a cabin by the creek in Grey Rock Valley – bin there more'n ten years.' He scratched his stubbly chin and added, 'I thought I'd give yuh a bit of advice.'

'About what?' Sally asked quietly.

''Bout the Double G – or what's left of it.'

Sally's expression sharpened as she felt she might be on the edge of learning something.

'It ain't the sort of advice you might take a-kindly to,' Tin Pan continued. 'Fact, I won't give it at all if you ain't the gal I'm a-lookin' fur. You're Sally Bradmore, ain't yuh?'

'Uh-huh,' Sally acknowledged. '*What* advice?' she asked urgently.

'Jest this... Don't yuh go a-sellin' what's left of th' Double G spread, or your mine.'

Tin Pan did not say any more. He turned abruptly and shuffled out of the store, leaving Sally staring after him in bewilderment. Then she shook her head and sighed. Obviously a local 'character' with much sun in the head. Perhaps, even, he *was* 'loco'! She turned back to her work again in a depressed mood, feeling that she had been let down badly when she had seemed to stand a chance of learning something.

She was still wondering about the old man when, towards six o'clock, she locked the doors of the store on the outside and prepared to depart for the hotel.

'Everythin' goin' OK?' asked Clem Billings' voice behind her, and she turned in surprise. He raised his Stetson and smiled at her.

'Oh, hello Mr Billings! Yes – everything's fine.'

'Good! I thought I'd picked the right gal to run the place.' Billings reflected. 'Look, I've gotten no nearer in findin' out what might have happened to your husband, but I have other ideas. How's about you an' me takin' a look at the ruins of your ranch?'

Sally shrugged. 'All right, but what good will it do? I've already been over it, and so has the sheriff. There are no clues to be found there.'

'Mebbe neither of you looked closely enough. It can't do any harm to look again.'

'Now?'

'If you can wait for a meal, yes. The light's good just now.'

Sally nodded and went to the back of the store for the pinto. Still in her workaday frock she mounted side-saddle and rode the frisky little animal to the front of the building where Billings was waiting for her, mounted on his powerful mare. Side by side they trotted leisurely up the high street and from it to the trail that led to Grey Rock Valley.

For part of the journey Sally was silent, her eyes travelling – this time with a more responsive appreciation – beyond the immediate glory of the brittle-bush fields to the mountain-sides, smothered with silvery white Apache plumes and stately wands of scarlet mallow. She could not help but think how much all this untamed beauty could mean to her if only she could find Ken...

'Thoughts not so good?' Clem Billings asked in concern.

'Just wondering about Ken,' she responded, sighing. 'And something else. It's been bothering me quite a lot, but since it concerns you I don't quite know how to put it.'

'Risk it,' Billings suggested.

'Well, I've been wondering, since you were Ken's neighbour, how it was you never noticed his ranch was on fire – why it was left to a lone puncher to see it.'

'Nothin' very mysterious about that,' the rancher responded. 'On the night of the fire I wasn't at home. I was over in Waterfall

Valley arrangin' a cattle deal. That explain it?'

'Yes, quite satisfactorily,' Sally assented, finding a good deal of suspicion lifted from her mind. 'I suppose it's queer, too, that Miss Alland at the other ranch didn't see anything either.'

'I can't answer for her,' Billings said, 'though I can try and find out for you. We're very good friends, Miss Alland and I.'

Sally nodded, but did not say any more. The leisurely ride out to the ruined Double G was completed at length, and Billings lifted her down from the saddle. Side by side they strolled into the blackened waste, all its stark, sombre tragedy illuminated by the brilliant early evening sun. Without commenting they explored the ruins from end to end, turning over charred logs and heaps of ashes, examining every little detail which offered the slightest hope of explanation – but the end of their examination found them no wiser than they had been at first.

'Reckon it's a waste of time after all, Mrs Bradmore,' Billings said quietly, looking down at her.

She nodded and gave a last look round. 'I suppose I'll have to gradually get used to the idea that Ken's gone for good.'

'Might make it easier for you to bear if you did,' Billings admitted. 'Tell you what might help, too – if you sold this land. I'd give you ten thousand for it. Considerin' it's a blackened waste with not a thing on it that's a fair price, as any lawyer will tell you if you like to enquire. I can add the land to my own and turn it to use – and you could certainly do with the money.'

'You're very generous to me, Mr Billings,' Sally said, with a faint smile. 'And it is an idea, too – but I'd like to think it over...' she hesitated.

'I think I understand,' Billings said. 'I guess you need to be perfectly satisfied in your own mind that Ken's dead before you do anythin'. Anyway, think it over: the offer stands at any time.'

'Thanks.'

Thoughtful, Sally walked with the big rancher and saloon-owner as far as the spot where the gates had been. He bestrode his mare and looked down at her.

'Think you can find your way back to town all right? I've urgent business to attend to at my ranch.'

'I'll be all right,' she assured him. 'Good-bye for now – and thanks again.'

He touched his hat and went riding away

into the glare of the sinking sun. Sally looked after him for a moment and then towards the rearing purple heights of the Pinga mountains. So much she had promised herself here, in this lush valley with its magnificent pastures...

'What did that jigger want? To buy yuh out?'

Sally started and twirled round. Leaning nonchalantly against one of the charred mesquite posts, his horse nibbling at roots a little distance away, was the old gold-prospector who had visited the store that morning. He eyed her pensively, his lids lowered in the sun-dazzle.

'Where did you come from?' Sally demanded, not sure whether to feel afraid.

He nodded vaguely in the direction of the mountains.

'I travel quiet. Bin keepin' my eye on yuh.'

'Then it's like your confounded impudence!' Sally declared angrily, going over to him. 'What's it got to do with you what I do? Who *are* you anyway, besides being a prospector? What do you want with me?'

'Jest want you t'come fer a ride. I'd have suggested it this mornin' only it weren't a good time with so many people around. Out here – an' I followed yuh from town – it's quiet. Nobody can see ... I figgered we'd go to my cabin,' he finished.

'Your cabin!'

Sally stared at him blankly for a moment, then turned on her heel in contempt, but before she could attempt to mount her pinto, Tin Pan spoke again.

'I asked yuh nicely,' he said, shaking his head in regret, 'but yuh don't seem to sabe. OK, Mrs Bradmore, now I'm *a-tellin'* yuh!'

His .45 was in his hand, steadily levelled. Still keeping it cocked on her, he slid on to his horse and rode over to her. She watched his actions in startled wonder.

'Git on your horse and go ahead of me,' he ordered; and as he saw the fear in her grey eyes he added, 'Don't go gittin' fancy notions into your head, gal. I know what I'm a-doin'... Go on – up yuh git!'

8

Since there was no alternative, Sally obeyed, and the old prospector, a drily amused grin on his leathery face, rode right behind her, directing the course she must take. It led away from the valley floor and its rich pasture land to rockier, more arid regions, until presently they were following an ancient arroyo strewn with a carpet of yellow primroses and whispering bells.

Sally estimated that they covered perhaps three miles, going ever deeper into the evening shadows cast by the mighty range, before she saw ahead of her a solitary cabin and, near it, a fast-moving stream which lost itself in the rocky wilderness.

The nearer they came to the cabin the more Sally racked her brains to think of a way of escape. She could not believe for a moment that the old man had any good motive for driving her alone into this waste. And if he really were mad anything might happen to her. She thought forlornly of the .38 she had left at the store.

'Kinda quiet around here, ain't it?' Tin Pan called to her, as he jogged along behind her.

She twisted her head sharply to look at him.

'What do you *want* with me?' she blazed at him. 'What sort of a game do you call this?'

'I reckon you'll find out soon enough.' He was quite unperturbed. 'That's where we stop.' He nodded to the cabin.

Sally studied it as they approached. It was constructed of rough, unpainted boards, and had a wide porch with untamed vines crawling round it. To one side of it, fenced in with thorny ocotillo, was a small and empty corral and a stable. In all other directions loomed the mountains, rearing in their invincible crags and buttresses to the dimming sky of cobalt-blue.

'OK,' Tin Pan said, when they had reached the porch. 'Git down.'

He slid from his horse and Sally did likewise, waiting as he pointed his gun. He waved it to the cabin's front door.

'Inside,' he instructed.

'I won't!' she retorted. 'I'll not have anything to do with this–'

'Gals c'n be the stupidest cusses,' he breathed, and grabbing her firmly under one arm he forced her up the two steps and kicked the cabin door open. She went stumbling in ahead of him as he released her.

Halting, she gazed round on a crudely furnished, almost bare, living-room.

'That door there,' the prospector said, and nodded to it.

Mystified she opened it and looked beyond. There was a slightly open window and the dim evening light was casting on a long-legged, fully dressed figure stretched on a crude bed. Round his head was a rough bandage.

'*Ken!*' Sally nearly screamed. '*Oh – Ken!*'

She plunged forward as the man looked up at her, and his big arms closed round her quivering shoulders. She kissed him once, twice, half a dozen times...

'Hey, ease up,' he gasped, half-laughing. 'Don't suffocate me! Gosh, Sal, but it's good to see you.'

'Ken...' She swallowed hard and dashed tears away from her eyes. 'You ... here, after all! And I'd given you up for dead!'

'But for Tin Pan I would have been,' he responded quietly. 'Here, sit down on the bed. I'm still a bit too rocky to sit up much.'

'I'll fix some coffee,' Tin Pan remarked from the doorway, holstering his gun as he grinned toothily. 'That's one stubborn wife you've gotten yerself, son,' he commented. 'I reckon she didn't trust an old buzzard like me drivin' her up into these mountains. Be danged if I blame her!'

He went out and closed the door. Sally sat on the edge of the bed, her emotional outburst subsiding. She studied her husband eagerly. He looked just as she had always

126

known him – lean-faced, grey-eyed, tanned with the burned-in brown of the outdoor man of the West. Over the bandage sprouted little curls of dark hair. Only his expression was drawn and exhausted. As she told him about his sister, and little William junior, he seemed to brighten considerably.

'So now I'm an uncle, eh? That's mighty good hearin', Sal!' He grinned. 'But what have you been doin'?' he questioned. 'Since you arrived back here and couldn't find me, I mean.'

'Been eating my heart out for you, Ken.' She added some of the details, skimping them. 'It's not what *I've* been doing,' she insisted. 'It's what happened to you and the ranch which counts.'

'I hardly know the facts myself, kid,' he answered moodily. 'On the night of the fire I went to bed a bit earlier than usual – before midnight anyway – so's to be ready for you, fresh as paint, next day. I woke up to find a gun diggin' in my ribs and somebody was tyin' me up – but good! I put up a fight and got a slug in the head. Next thing I knew I was here. Tin Pan had taken out the bullet, which fortunately for me was only lodging in the front of my skull.'

'I'd bin to the Blue Dollar an' was takin'

my time comin' home,' Tin Pan commented, coming in with the coffee and hearing Ken's last sentence. 'I saw th' fire at the Double G an' a gang of about six ridin' like hell down the valley trail! So I thought I'd take a look-see. Reckon it wus as well I did. I found Ken all hog tied and unconscious. I got him out and brought him here – fixed him up. Ain't the fust time I've dug a bullet out. Dug 'em outa me own hide many a time.'

He grinned again, threw his coonskin hat on a chair, and poured out coffee for three into tin cups.

'And I thought you were a ... well, I don't know what!' Sally exclaimed. 'Can you ever forgive me, Tin Pan?'

'Oh, sure,' he chuckled, handing the coffee over. 'I reckon I do look like sump'n the buzzards got at. Livin' here alone all these years I reckon y'don't git to carin' how yuh look... Anyway, once this husband of yourn recovered he told me about his wife – and that weren't until last night, when he'd gotten over his delirium. I figgered I'd better start a-lookin' for yuh. I had t'be careful, though. It were obvious somebody had figgered on gittin' Ken outa the way, an' his ranch with him, an' I didn't want to betray that he wus at th' cabin. So I jest fished around, got t'know where you wus, and waited my chance to bring yuh here without attractin' attention. I figger that's all there is to it.'

'Neither of us can ever be grateful enough for all you've done, Tin Pan,' Ken said earnestly.

'Aw shucks, it ain't nothin'.' The old prospector almost looked embarrassed. 'Y'can both stay here if yuh want. I'd be glad of company.'

Sally pondered seriously for some moments as she drank her coffee; then she frowned.

'Just who is at the back of all this, Ken? You must have some idea.'

'Pity of it is, Sal, I haven't,' he muttered. 'As far as I know I haven't any enemies. The whole thing's a complete mystery to me. You, Tin Pan, say that you saw six riders. For the life of me I can't figure out who they could have been, or why they did what they did.'

'Well now, I don't know who they wus, else I'd ha' told th' sheriff,' Tin Pan said, scratching his whiskery chin and thinking. 'But I've a mighty good idea what it's all about – an' soon as you're fit I'll show yuh, an' th' gal.'

'Do you think Ken's life is still in danger?'

Sally asked sharply.

'I reckon it will be if he's seen – that's sort of obvious, ain't it? Right now, whoever done it thinks he died in th' fire as planned an' they'll a-go right on thinkin' it as long as yuh stay here, Ken.'

'But I can't stay here for ever!' he protested. 'I want to be knowing what all this is about, find out who's back of it.'

'I'll show yuh what it's all about soon as yuh c'n sit on a cayuse without fallin' off. Then yuh can figger out fer yourself who's got a bead on yuh.'

'This means I've got to return to my hotel,' Sally said. 'If I miss being there Mr Billings will start searching for me, perhaps, and may get this far.'

'Billings...?' Ken mused with his eyes narrowed. 'Just wonder if he fits in on this?'

'He told me he's become a friend of yours as well as a neighbour,' Sally remarked.

'Yeah – which is true, up to a point. But he offered ten thousand, you say, for that blackened waste! It's a tidy sum.'

'I got the impression he made the offer from generosity,' Sally responded, reflecting. 'Matter of fact, I think he believes he has a chance of getting to know me much better since he thinks you are dead.'

'I warned yuh this mornin' 'bout sellin',' Tin Pan pointed out. 'An' I meant it. Don't sell at any price, 'cos that, t' my way of thinkin', is what's back of this whole set up.'

'Look,' Ken implored, 'why don't you come into the open, Tin Pan? What's so valuable about my property and land that a gang of owl-hooters should want to kill me and burn the spread for? I lived on the Double G for this past year and never saw anythin' unusual about it. Good pastures, but that's about all. And I've examined the mine again myself and didn't find any sign of gold.'

'There's still sump'n else yuh don't know about,' Tin Pan said grimly. 'But I want yuh t' see it with your own eyes. In fact, I'd've told th' sheriff 'bout it long ago, but seein' as it wus on your land I sort of never got around to it.'

Ken struggled into a sitting position and then held his head tightly and winced. Sally caught his arm.

'Ken, dearest, take it easy! You're not fit to–'

'I'm all right,' he insisted stubbornly. 'What I need is some fresh air. I want to know what you're talkin' about, Tin Pan, and I want to know tonight!'

The old prospector mused for a moment and then nodded. 'OK, I reckon that head o' yourn 'll be all right once you've some decent food inside yuh. I'll rustle up a meal fer th' three of us, then we'll take a ride an' I'll show yuh jest what I mean.'

An hour later, with the night completely fallen, and Ken still insisting that he was quite fit enough to ride – the trio left the cabin, Tin Pan using the girl's pinto and she sitting in front of Ken in the prospector's horse's saddle. Being the larger animal it was able to cope with a double mount.

'It ain't too fur,' Tin Pan said. 'Mebbe a couple of miles. Jest follow me – an' watch yourself with these rocks.'

Ken and Sally said nothing, simply obeying. Dark though it was, the brilliant stars cast a faint illumination, picking out an almost disused trail leading tortuously through the midst of rocky spurs, across small freshets, or amidst the dense inter-lacings of cedar- and juniper-trees. The air smelled cold, blowing down in heady draughts from the heights of the mountains, but it was refreshing too, and stirred Ken to a new strength as he urged the horse gently onwards.

'There ain't no critter in North Wind knows what I know,' Tin Pan said after a while, and seemed sardonically pleased with the fact. 'I've washed dirt around this region fer so long there ain't no part of it I don't...'

He stopped, simultaneously with the whanging sound of a bullet. The pinto he was riding shied, throwing him from the saddle. Ken's horse reared in fright and tossed Sally, riding sideways, into the dust. Ken dropped down after her, helping her up – and another bullet slashed the rocky wall of the trail. He realized in that moment that had he and Sally been in the saddle one of them would certainly have received that second bullet. Grimly he listened to the echoing beat of a horse's hoofs fast retreating down the rocky trail into the night.

'Tin Pan–!' Sally gasped. 'Do you think...?'

Ken drove forward, with her following quickly behind him. On his knees, Ken lifted up the fallen prospector and felt his breast hurriedly. Dimly visible on the face was a streak of blood.

'They got him, Sal,' Ken whispered, his voice quivering with fury. 'Clean through the head by the looks of it.'

'But who?' Sally demanded, staring blindly into the dark.

'No time to ask ourselves that,' Ken said curtly. 'Here – you take the pinto. I'll carry Tin Pan on the horse. The next person we've got to see is Sheriff Garson.'

He hauled the dead prospector's body on to his shoulder and took him to the horse's saddle, draping him across it. Then, with his Colt drawn ready for action, he urged the horse back along the trail, Sally following up in the rear, and so finally, without any further manifestations of attack, they regained the cabin.

Once he had deposited the body on the bed, Ken came back into the living-room to find that Sally had lighted the solitary oil-lamp. She was looking at him with wide, frightened grey eyes.

'If only we knew what it was all about!' she exclaimed. 'It's so – so ghastly! This shooting to kill without there being any reason we know of.'

Ken's face was grim. 'And now Tin Pan's dead I guess we'll never know the reason, 'less we hit on it by accident.'

Sally settled on a chair and rubbed her forehead wearily.

'One thing seems pretty certain, anyway,'

she said. 'That second shot tonight was aimed at us, and it'd have got one of us if the horse hadn't shied. That means that whoever was firing knows that you're not dead – so you don't have to hide yourself any more.'

Ken sat down too, elbows on the rough table, and pushed his dusty sombrero up on to his forehead.

'Yeah, that makes sense,' he agreed. 'It also means that you and Tin Pan must have been followed back to the cabin here this evening by somebody, and once we stepped out that person tried to get us. That somebody isn't an amateur with a gun, either – firin' dead shots with only the starlight. That sounds like professional bushwhackers who do little else but use a gun. But *why?* That's the thing that has us stymied, Sal.'

'I still keep thinking about our abandoned gold-mine,' she said thoughtfully. 'Supposing it's not played out after all? Our ranch is perched over a bonanza and we don't know it, but somebody else does? Remember how Boyd Wilcot tried to buy it from Dad?'

'That would make things logical if there *was* gold,' he answered her, 'but there isn't. I've examined the mine, don't forget. All I found was the dead body of Jack Andrews, which Wilcot had hidden there – that had to be the reason he tried to buy it ... to stop anyone finding the body. There isn't gold, and there isn't oil – not even a buried watercourse, which might be worth somethin'...' Ken rubbed the back of his neck in perplexity. 'I'm just bushwhacked when it comes to figurin' out the reason, Sal. But, back of it all, I can't help keep thinking about Billings. He *did* make an offer, and that thought kinda sticks. Ten thousand greenbacks for pastureland which he'll have to work up and add to his own is a mighty large sum.'

'Just the same, I don't feel suspicious about him,' Sally insisted. 'He's been decent to me, and always correct in his manners.'

Ken gave a sardonic grin. 'You don't know Clem Billings like I do. These days he's a big man around these parts – saloon- and property-owner, gambler, and now cattle dealer. A man in this region doesn't get to be all those things by shootin' an unloaded dice every time. As for him bein' my friend, he was never that. Just a neighbour – no more an' no less. Anyway,' he added grimly, 'this has gotten down now to cold-blooded murder, and that's a job for the sheriff. I'm going to him right now – and you're coming with me. It's not safe to leave you here.

Since our enemies know I'm alive I'm quittin' this hole-and-corner business right now. Let's go.'

9

It was several hours later. Sheriff Garson, once he had gotten over his shock at seeing Ken alive, had ridden out with them and collected Tin Pan's body. Now he had returned to town, leaving Ken and the girl to themselves. They considered each other over a meal in the lamplight, pondering upon what the sheriff had had to say.

'We may get somethin' out of it; we may not,' Ken sighed. 'He's taken Tin Pan's body into town, where the bullet'll be removed and sent to Phoenix for expert examination. After that, since there's no other evidence, it's a matter of finding the gun which fired that particular bullet – and that'll be as easy as catching a swift on the wing. I know I did it with Boyd Wilcot once before but that was because I already had reason to suspect him. This time we've no real suspects.'

'And that's all the law can do?' Sally asked dispiritedly.

'I reckon so. How else can the murderer be found? As for the attack on me, in spite of all the sheriff's promises, I don't see how he's ever goin' to find the six who did it... We've done all we can, Sal,' he finished seriously, 'and I'm almighty sorry that our resumption of married life had to start in this all-fired way.'

She patted his brown hand as it lay on the table. 'Oh, we'll get by somehow, Ken. You'll see.'

'It means that our lives will be in constant danger,' he warned her. 'I'm thinkin' I should send word to Bill Winslow and tell him what's happened. With him and some of his Straight H boys helpin' us–'

'We're not going to do that!' Sally declared. 'I've already been through all that in my own mind before now. Supposing Bill got killed trying to help us, and we left his baby son without a father? What would your sister Emily think of us then?'

Ken shook his head ruefully. 'Sorry Sal, guess I wasn't thinkin' straight. You're right, of course.'

'We're going to try and find things out for *ourselves*,' Sally said decisively. 'Even if we do make ourselves targets for gunmen by so doing. We've just *got* to find out the reason for everything. Tomorrow I think we should go to what remains of the ranch and you can decide how much it will cost to rebuild it. Since we still own the land it's the logical thing to do.'

'Yeah – risks or no risks,' he admitted. 'And what about you and your general store job?'

'I quit that the moment I found you – as I'll explain to Mr Billings when I see him. He'll understand.'

'What money I had was in the ranch,' Ken said slowly. 'And it wasn't in a safe, either – so I reckon it's ashes now. We're cleaned out, Sal, and it's only right you should know it in case you think you can do better for yourself by keeping on at that store job.'

She smiled, got up from her chair and came round to him. She kissed him gently.

'I'm not doing that. The pioneers started from scratch and so can we. That being settled we'd better think about turning in, hadn't we? You've done quite enough for a convalescent.'

They made their preparations for retiring and, though both of them were alert at intervals throughout the night, nothing disturbed the peace. The dawn came up behind the mountains in a splendour of liquid gold, and deepening warmth pouring into the mountain canyon set the gathered mists stirring like a giant's garment.

From Tin Pan's small stock of food Ken and Sally breakfasted, and then with the pinto and horse they set out along the trail for the ruined Double G. They kept on the watch all the time, Sally with one of Ken's twin Colts and he with the other; but there were no evidences of being pursued and even less of shots.

Half an hour later they had left the mountain territory behind and had the valley floor spread before them – Beatrice Alland's ranch to the left, Billings' to the right, and their own blackened spread in the centre.

In another ten minutes they had gained it. Ken wandered through the midst, assessing the damage, and Sally waited for him on the pinto. She took her attention from him as two riders came up. Instinctively she reached for the Colt in the saddle holster and then relaxed, beholding Clem Billings on his mare, and beside him on a sorrel was a slim, dark-headed girl in riding-skirt and silk blouse, a vermilion kerchief at her throat.

'Hello, Mr Billings,' Sally greeted, smiling. 'I'm glad you came up. I was coming to your ranch later to tell you that I'm through with the store. You see–'

'I can see why! You found Ken,' Billings acknowledged, looking at the tall, lean figure prowling in the debris. 'That's mighty good knowin', Mrs Bradmore. Sorry to lose you and I'll send payment to date to your hotel. Where was Ken hidin'?'

'Er – up in the mountains.'

The rancher's dark eyes had further questions in them, but he did not utter them. Instead he glanced at the good-looking girl beside him.

'This is your neighbour, Mrs Bradmore – Miss Alland of the Treble Circle, further up the valley yonder.'

'How are you?' Beatrice Alland acknow-ledged, rather coldly.

Sally was about to speak when Ken came up. He eyed Billings narrowly and then touched his hat to Beatrice Alland.

'Mornin', Miss Alland,' he greeted; and switched back to Billings. 'What's the idea, Clem, of tryin' to buy up my land the moment you thought I was dead?'

The other smiled. 'Why not? Sensible thing, wasn't it? Your wife was cleaned out an' in a pretty hopeless situation. I thought it was the right thing to do.'

'Sure you had no other reason?'

Billings' smile faded. 'What other reason *would* I have? You aimin' to get tough about it?'

'Mebbe. A guy gets to bein' suspicious when owl-hooters put a slug in his head and then start burnin' his spread down. Even more so when somebody offers more'n the land's worth only a few days after.'

'Be suspicious if you want,' Billings shrugged. 'I'm not interested any more now you're back... So you reckon that owl-hooters did it all, do you?'

'I *know* they did. Six of them. Thought they'd got me, but they weren't thorough enough.'

The dark brown eyes of Beatrice Alland strayed from Sally's pretty face to Ken's determined one. She asked a question in her languid, cultivated voice.

'And what do you hope to do with this ruin now, Mr Bradmore? With all the cattle gone and just ashes remaining it's a bit hopeless, isn't it?'

'I'm planning to start over,' he replied. 'I'll get fresh cattle and rebuild the ranch ... somehow. I've done it once: I can do it again.'

'That will take money,' the girl rancher said. 'Plenty of it, too. Then you'll need an outfit of boys to look after—'

'I don't need an outfit,' Ken interrupted. 'What there is to do I can do myself same as before. As for money – there'll be a way.'

'There are only two ways,' Beatrice Alland told him. 'You either steal or gamble.'

'Right,' Billings confirmed.

'What gave you the idea I'd want to steal?' Ken asked drily.

The woman shrugged and looked at Clem Billings.

'We'd better be on our way,' she said. 'We're probably holding you up, Mr Bradmore – and, anyway, we've our morning ride to finish.'

Ken nodded, and Sally watched the two ride away slowly into the sunlight. Then she glanced at Ken.

'Apparently,' she commented, 'Miss Alland is something of a sophisticate.'

'Oh, she's all right,' Ken growled. 'Got large ideas, though, since she became the boss of the Treble Circle. It's *Billings* I don't like. I'm pretty sure he had something to do with all this.'

'Well, since we can't prove it, what's the practical thing to do? Get money?'

'I reckon so.' Ken glanced at the ruins. 'Take at least eight thousand dollars to fix this up – and Miss Alland had the right idea when she said gambling's the only way to do it. I'm a pretty good poker-player. It's getting the stake-money to begin with that has me worried.'

'It needn't,' Sally smiled. 'I've still my bit by me, remember. Would two hundred dollars start you off?'

'Sure would – but there's always the chance I might lose it.'

'Since we don't seem to be doing anything else but take chances I'll risk it. Let's ride on to my hotel and I'll pick up my things and get the money at the same time...'

So at sundown that evening Sally and Ken entered the Blue Dollar to find it warming up to its usual thickly clogged atmosphere. Both of them were prepared for anything that might happen, but apparently none of the punchers or cattlemen present seemed particularly interested in them. One or two of the women, recognizing Sally again now she was in riding-skirt and shirt, eyed her jealously for a moment and then looked away.

'OK,' Ken murmured, gripping the girl's arm. 'Here's where I do my best – and I don't think there could be anybody better to play than Clem Billings himself.'

He nodded to where Billings was seated playing cards at a distant corner-table, his black Stetson pushed up on his forehead and a glass of beer at his side.

Sally gave a doubting glance. 'Isn't that rather asking for it? He's a professional gambler, isn't he? Can't you find somebody less experienced?'

'Sure,' Ken grinned, 'but none of them with the money he's got! I want eight thousand dollars, remember, and that's a stake only Billings can put up. If I lose...' Ken looked grim for a moment. 'We'll tackle that afterwards. Come on.'

They went across to where Billings was seated, then they realized that Beatrice Alland was present too, still in her riding-clothes. She sat smoking pensively, a little distance from the table, watching the game. Her dark eyebrows rose a trifle when Sally and Ken came into view.

'Well, well, the battling Bradmores,' she commented drily.

'Evening, Miss Alland – howdy, Clem,' Ken said. 'I'm feelin' like a game.'

'So you can get back in the cattle racket?' Billings smiled. 'Okay. Blow, you!' he added to the man with whom he had been playing. 'Go an' keep Cal Reynolds company. Looks as if he needs it.'

The man shuffled off and joined the dissolute *hombre* Billings had named at a nearby table.

'I hope you know Clem's the best player hereabouts,' Beatrice Alland remarked.

'I know it,' Ken answered. 'And I'm not scared, neither.'

Smoke drifted from the woman's nostrils. 'Please yourself. I'm just warning you. How about you, Mrs Bradmore? Think you can stand the strain?'

'I've stood worse,' Sally answered, and sat down near the woman to watch.

Round the table a little group quickly gathered. When Clem Billings really set out to play poker he was worth watching.

'Two hundred ante to start with,' Ken said, and staked his chips. Billings nodded and then dealt out the cards. The game began.

For two reasons Ken played with some confidence. He knew that Billings, as a player, never cheated; and he was sure of his own ability, given a little luck, to beat him – and at first he did. Then he began to lose before a straight, a triplet, and a straight flush.

'Sort of bears out the old adage, doesn't it?' Beatrice Alland asked, as during a grim pause Ken reckoned up his dwindling finances.

'About what?' Billings asked, round his cheroot.

'Lucky at cards, unlucky at love. You're certainly not unlucky at cards, Clem.'

Ken glanced up, his blue eyes narrowed at Beatrice Alland.

'Meanin' what?' he asked shortly.

'You didn't know?' The woman looked at him in surprise. 'Why, had you not turned up again I do believe Clem here would have asked this golden-haired wife of yours to marry him – even to pushing me on one side if necessary.'

'That's a damned lie!' Billings snapped. 'All I tried to do for Mrs Bradmore was–'

'Yeah, I'd like to know just what you *did* do for my wife,' Ken snapped, jumping up. 'She was fooled into thinkin' that you meant nothin' by helping her, but I think there was a price behind it, had you gotten around to it – an' if I hadn't turned up.' His hand reached out and seized Billings' coat lapel, dragging him up from his chair. 'I've never really liked you, Clem – an' I like you still less right now. Mebbe I should get some of the dislike out of my system, huh?'

'Ken, stop it! Please!' Sally implored.

'Oh, don't disturb them, Mrs Bradmore,' Beatrice Alland commented languidly. 'It won't be the first time two men have fought over a woman.'

'I'm not fighting!' Billings snapped. 'There's no need to! I tell you I...'

Ken did not give him the chance to finish. Inflamed with what he felt sure was quite justifiable suspicion he lashed out a savage uppercut. It struck Billings on the chin, slewed him round, and he fell across the table, carrying chips and cards along with him.

He was up again almost immediately, lunging out with his massive fists. Ken dodged the worst blows, swung round a haymaker, missed, and fell on the floor. Immediately Billings was on top of him and they fought and struggled furiously with each other, the men and women watching expanding or contracting the circle they made to give room.

It was a vicious jab in the face that finally settled Billings. Breathing hard, he lay flat and Ken slowly straightened up.

'Stick to your own women in future,' he

breathed. 'And you can keep your rotten poker-game, too...' He flung the cards down on top of the dazed Billings. 'I'll figure out another way to get money. Come on, Sal.'

He had time to notice that her pretty face was flushed and angry, but he did not question it there and then. Pushing her ahead of him, he strode out of the saloon and into the cool night air. Breathing hard, he straightened his kerchief and scooped back his hair under his sombrero.

'Ken Bradmore, you're a damned fool!' Sally declared angrily. 'Just how much good did it do you to tackle Clem Billings that way?'

'All the good in the world. It relieved my feelings!'

'All you really did was make an exhibition of yourself,' she retorted. 'It was only that chance remark on Miss Alland's part which started you off. Clem Billings *never* made himself objectionable to me. He only helped me, all along the line.'

'In time he'd have wanted payment – of a kind.' Ken's face was grim. 'I know the kind of a guy he is.'

'You've made an enemy of him, Ken, and that doesn't help. And maybe of Miss Alland too, since she seems to be in love with him.

If we ever get the ranch going again we'll have two neighbours who hate us. *If* we ever get going,' Sally repeated. 'All you've done is throw away the money I gave you.'

'There'll be some other way,' Ken muttered, and he led the way from the saloon's boardwalk to the two horses at the hitch rail. 'After all, Sal, I was only thinking of you, and I had a vision of what that swine Billings *might* have done.' He caught hold of her and lifted her into the saddle. 'Forget it,' he said. 'Let's get back to the cabin. Guess it'll do as a place to live for now.'

Throughout most of the journey back down the valley trail in the starlight Sally did not say anything, and Ken stole a curious glance at her once or twice. They had reached the cabin again before her thoughts found words.

'Just what *are* we going to do, Ken? That two hundred dollars you lost before the fight started was about all I'd got. Without money what happens next? You can't even gamble when you've no cash to put up a stake.'

'We'll probably have to hit the trail,' Ken said, lifting her down from the pinto. 'Perhaps go to Glover City or some other nearby town, and I'll find work there, or something.

Be safer, too, since somebody's still on the prod for us. Then when we've got some money again we'll come back and tackle the ranch. No other way.'

'And if in the meantime the ranch is used by whoever is trying to get hold of it?'

'That we'll have to risk – though I don't see how that could be. The sheriff would put a stop to that.'

'You hope! The kind of desperadoes we're fighting don't seem as though they'd let a sheriff worry them! If only we knew what it was Tin Pan had been meaning to tell us.'

'We don't – and that's that,' Ken sighed. 'Go on inside, Sal; I'll stable the horses. We'll discuss this thing in the morning. Maybe we'll see things clearer after a sleep.'

10

In the small hours Ken suddenly awoke. In any case his sleeping had been fitful, partly through worry as to his future prospects, and partly for fear of possible attack either from Billings, of whom he felt sure he had now made an enemy, or from the mysterious gunman who seemed determined to end his life and that of the girl sleeping peacefully by his side.

For a moment or two he lay listening, wondering what had aroused him; then he distinctly heard the closing of the cabin's front door. Immediately he got out of the bed, moving silently on bootless feet towards the window. There was a dim, solitary figure visible on the porch in the starlight, a horse fastened to the porch rail.

Ken turned back swiftly into the room and dragged on his boots. He was fully dressed – since he had no other clothes – except for his gunbelt. Buckling it on he looked thoughtfully at the dim figure of Sally, then, at the sound of speeding hoofs on the night air, he left the room and sped through the adjoining room and on to the porch.

The unknown intruder was riding away down the canyon trail, though not at a particularly great speed. To get his horse from the stable and saddle it did not take Ken above three minutes; then he sped in the direction the visitor had taken – catching sight of him in the starlight some five minutes afterwards.

Realizing he was being followed the rider put on speed, but Ken kept steadily on his track, one of his Colts drawn as he rode. He was ready to blast the man from his horse the moment he had the chance, then hand him over to the sheriff as a trespasser.

Only he did not get the chance. The man rode hard, and well, emerging presently from the canyon trail into the wide sweep of the valley side. Here he turned due right, speeding through the valley in the dim light, with Ken doing his utmost to catch him up, and failing. When at last they had reached the end of the valley the man's faster horse gave him the advantage and he drew away into the night, vanishing in the mist-covered vastness of the pastureland. Ken drew his mount to a halt and holstered his gun.

'Reckon we lost him, feller,' he murmured to the snorting horse. 'Never mind; you did your best anyway.'

Puzzling to himself as to the reason for the night visit – and that he and Sally had escaped untouched in spite of it – he returned as rapidly as he could to the cabin. He found the oil-lamp lighted and a worried girl pacing up and down in the glow.

'What on earth happened to you?' she demanded, as he came in from the porch. 'I woke up and found you'd gone. I've been worried sick.'

'Sorry, Sal, but I saw no point in waking you.' He told her briefly what had happened, and she stared at him amazedly.

'Who on earth could it have been? What did he want?'

'You're as wise as I am. Obviously not to kill us, because he had the opportunity and didn't take it. The only thing I can think of is that he came to steal something, though what there'd be in this cabin worth stealin' I'll be darned if I know. And there's nothing of ours here.'

They began a search, until they realized the futility of it. Since they had no real idea what the cabin contained they had no way of knowing if anything had been stolen.

'Maybe somebody hoping to find Tin Pan – some saddle tramp,' Sally suggested. 'He found Tin Pan wasn't here and so just rode away again.'

'Then why didn't he stop and let me catch him up? He made darned sure I got nowhere near him.'

They looked at each other, baffled.

'We'd better finish our sleep,' Sally decided finally, yawning behind her hand. 'This business doesn't make sense...'

But it started to the following morning. She and Ken had just finished a breakfast of baked beans and coffee when the glow of morning sunlight through the open doorway of the cabin was darkened by the form of Sheriff Garson and one of his deputies. There was no mistaking the grim expression on his tanned face.

'Howdy, Sheriff,' Ken greeted, and Sally nodded to him. 'Early caller, aren't you?'

'With reason.' Garson stopped beside the table, his deputy taking up a stand by the door.

'Is there something wrong?' Sally asked uneasily. 'I can't help but think there must be, to bring you all this way out here.'

'Yeah, there's something wrong,' the sheriff agreed; then his eyes turned to Ken again. 'This morning, Ken, a cattle-dealer came to my office the moment it was open an' reported a hold-up of the night-stage from Antelope. It was carryin' some gold-dust through to Springville, stopping at North Wind on the way. The dust was worth around twenty thousand dollars. The hold-up man took it. The stage driver also reported it. The thief was masked, an' about your build – what could be seen of him in the starlight.'

Ken stared fixedly. 'Well? So what?'

'The cattle-dealer was ridin' the trail solo and saw the whole thing happen. He followed the outlaw, unknown to him, and he came right here – to this cabin. So,' Garson finished grimly, 'I'm thinkin' you owe me an explanation, Ken.'

Ken clenched his fists on the table. 'Now I begin to get it,' he breathed. 'That guy in the night who came here–'

'What guy?' the sheriff interrupted. He listened while Ken gave him the facts. Then he glanced at Sally. 'This right, Mrs Bradmore?'

'I – I suppose so, Sheriff. I woke up to find Ken gone, and he told me about the stranger when he got back.'

'Uh-huh.' Garson ran a finger over his lips. 'Any idea why a hold-up man should want to come here, Ken – of all places?'

'No idea at all, but I'll wager he was the same man.'

'I'll take a look around,' the sheriff decided, and with his deputy he began a hole-and-corner examination of the cabin, his deputy helping him, whilst Ken and Sally watched in grim silence.

It was perhaps ten minutes later when a loose section of board caught Garson's attention. He raised it, looked below, and drew two bags into view. He dumped them on the table, where Sally and Ken stared at them incredulously. They were even more incredulous when they saw the yellow dust inside them.

'S'pose you tell me, Ken, why an outlaw leaves his loot here?' Garson demanded. 'It isn't logical, to my way of thinkin'.'

'But dammit, man, you don't think *I* did it?'

'You were out in the night, weren't you? Nobody's seen this supposed stranger you're talkin' about 'cept you. Not even your wife.'

'But I don't know anythin' about this gold-dust!' Ken jumped up angrily. 'Look, this is a frame-up of some sort! That man came here to plant this gold and then switched the blame to me. I never robbed a stage in my life. Why should I?'

'There's a good enough reason this time. It's pretty general gossip in town that you gambled your last two hundred dollars away last night an' that you need money bad. You could have found out beforehand about the stage.' Before Ken could speak the sheriff's gun was pointing at him. 'Sorry, Ken, I've the law to enforce,' he said quietly. 'Hand over your gunbelts.'

Ken obeyed, handing them over the rough table.

'So you're arrestin' me, Garson? That it? And I thought we were friends!'

'I'm sorry, Ken. I have to put my job before my personal feelings. Facts are things I can't get behind. Outside – and get on your horse. I'm runnin' you in on suspicion until I've gotten more evidence–'

'But my wife!' Ken burst out. 'I can't leave her! Our lives seem to be threatened even as it is. Without me to protect her anything might happen! You know already that we only just escaped death the other night.'

'You'll ride into town with us, Mrs Bradmore,' Garson told her. 'Get together your things, if you've got any, and put up again at the hotel where you were. You'll be safe enough there; I'll have an eye to you.'

'Sheriff, Ken didn't do this thing!' Sally insisted. 'You just can't take the evidence of a stray cattle-dealer!'

'These two bags are mighty strong evidence,' Garson answered. 'An' if that cattle-man's lyin' he's mighty barefaced about it. He hasn't quit town. He's stayin' at Ma Brayson's roomin' house, where I can question him any time I want. Can't see what reason he'd have for lyin', anyway.'

He broke off and moved his gun impatiently.

'Let's be on our way,' he ordered.

Taking up her old room again at the Hillview Hotel, and finding that in the interval Clem Billings had left her salary to date in a sealed envelope, to be called for, Sally spent most of the morning thinking out what she should do next. That the whole thing was a plant and that Ken was speaking the truth she never doubted for an instant – but how to find out the truth was a problem which baulked her. And there was worse to come. Towards midday Sheriff Garson called upon her.

She showed him into her small room and regarded him worriedly as he pulled off his hat and studied her with sombre eyes.

'Afraid I've bad news, Mrs Bradmore,' he said.

'About Ken?' Sally looked startled. 'Why, what has he–'

'Oh, nothin' has happened to him. He's safely tucked away in the jail at the back of my office – but I've had to alter the charge against him to ... murder!'

'What! Whom ... did he murder?'

'Ephriam Millthorn – better known as Tin Pan.'

Sally sat down on the edge of the bed, her

head spinning.

'But that's impossible! Tin Pan befriended us. We were going along the trail with him when somebody shot–'

'Yes, Mrs Bradmore, I know your story, and Ken's.' Garson looked down on her in quiet sympathy. 'I'm mighty sorry to have to pile it on this thick: a sheriff's job is tough sometimes. But I've got the bullet back from Phoenix – the one that killed Tin Pan. The striker-pin indent on it was made by Ken's left-hand Colt. There's no doubt about it. I fired a test bullet from Ken's left-hand Colt, and the imprint is the same. I've sent both bullets to Phoenix for a check-up, but there's no doubt in my mind. When I saw the queer striker mark I saw too, on examining Ken's guns, that one Colt has a queer striker pin, slightly damaged. The way it looks from that evidence, Ken fired the bullet which killed Tin Pan.'

'And what does Ken say?' Sally could hardly utter the words.

'He denies that it is his gun. He says that, like most of us, he doesn't use his left-hand Colt nearly as much as his right – that his own left-hand Colt had been taken and the murder-gun put in its place – somewhere, sometime. He also reminded me that he himself had handed me similar evidence last year–'

'Yes – about Wilcot!' Sally snapped. 'Do you think Ken would be stupid enough to overlook the same thing about himself?'

'Guess it is kinda ironical, at that.' Garson looked troubled, then he shook his head. 'I'm really sorry to have to...'

'That's all right, Sheriff, you're only doing your duty,' she said, getting up. 'I've a plan of my own I'd like to try. I think I know when that gun was switched. Anyway, I'm going to try and find out. If I get real evidence you'll act, won't you?'

'Naturally. And,' the Sheriff added, as he pulled the door open, 'I hope you get it. I don't like havin' to do this sort of thing to Ken and you.'

He picked up his hat and departed, leaving Sally staring in front of her. Eventually she made up her mind, left the hotel, and went down to her pinto in the hotel's livery stable. Less than an hour later she was hammering on the screen door of Clem Billings' ranch house, and to her satisfaction he himself came to open it.

'Well, Mrs Bradmore!' He gazed at her in pleased astonishment. 'This is one big surprise. Come right in... You were lucky to catch me. Just had my lunch and was setting off for–'

'I've a very urgent reason for being here, Mr Billings,' Sally interrupted. 'I want to talk to you in private.'

'Sure thing. Go ahead in.'

He waved her into a large, log-walled, well-furnished living-room, then motioned to a chair. Taking up a stand by the mantel he looked at her, still in some wonder.

'What's the trouble? I left your money at the hotel…'

'I know – and thanks.' Sally hesitated.

'What then? Where's your husband?'

'Under arrest, for holding up the night stage from Antelope and stealing two bags of gold-dust. He's also accused of murdering a prospector known as Tin Pan.'

'Tin Pan? *That* old buzzard?' And as Billings stared incredulously, so Sally gave him all the details.

'Why, the thing's idiotic!' he declared flatly. 'Ken may be a hot-tempered critter – as f'r instance when he sailed into me in the Blue Dollar, but he's not an outlaw or a murderer.' He gave a rueful grin. 'I don't hold that fight we had against him, y'know. He just didn't stop to think, I reckon … I haven't been into town this mornin' else I'd have heard about the stage hold-up and his arrest. So – how do I fit in?'

Sally looked at him steadily.

'Mr Billings, I've had quite a battle with myself weighing you up,' she said quietly. 'I've tried all along to convince myself that you're a gentleman, and honest – but I can't do it any more. At least I don't think you're honest. I believe *you* have gotten Ken into this mess.'

Billings' grin faded and the incredulous look returned.

'I have? For why?'

'Because you've taken a fancy to me. Let's not beat about the bush. Had Ken not been found you'd have done just what he said – have made advances to me, and I might even have accepted you. But he turned up again and squashed all that. So you decided to have a second try – to get him out of the way for good, by pinning an outlawry and murder charge on him, so – you hope – being able to have me when he has been hanged!'

Billings rubbed his chin. 'I like you, Sal,' he admitted, dropping all formality, 'but I stopped thinkin' about you when Ken reappeared. So help me, I never dug up such a scheme in my life! I'm not blamin' you for thinkin' of it because you're pretty worried. But it's crazy... Quite crazy.'

'I don't think it is. Ken swears that his guns were switched, to ensure him getting the one that killed Tin Pan. That transfer could only have taken place when he *was* in company, and the only time he was in company was when he fought you in the Blue Dollar. I think you started that fight on purpose to give somebody a chance to switch the guns. It could have been done. You knew he was intending to gamble, sooner or later. You had the chance to fix everything.'

'Determined to think the worst of me, aren't you?' Billings asked bitterly. 'Supposin' you're right – which you're not – what do you expect me to do now?'

'Clear Ken by bringing to justice the man who switched the guns, and, possibly, the same man who robbed the stage and planted the gold-dust in the cabin. I believe you know who that man is. You can do it, without involving yourself. I don't believe you committed the actual crimes, but I *do* believe you're back of them, even to burning down the Double G.'

'Still wrong,' Billings said, lighting a cheroot, then he became pensive. 'Just the same. I see what you mean about the gun switch. Could have been done as we fought. Let me think now: who was lookin' on...?'

He stood for several minutes, thinking hard; then he asked a question:

'Who's this cattle-dealer who's given information about the hold-up?'

'I don't know anything about him, beyond the fact that he's staying on in town, at Ma Brayson's rooming house.'

'He is, huh?' Billings seemed to make up his mind. 'Tell you what I'll do, Sally – I think I can prove Ken's innocence, for a price.'

'Price! For something *you* did?'

'I *didn't* do it, believe it or not! As for the price, I want your Double G land in return for Ken's freedom!'

11

Sally stared at Billings for a moment and then got to her feet in indignation.

'Never in this world!' she declared flatly.

'All right... If you think that blackened

waste and played-out mine is more important to you than Ken's life, that's your worry.
I've made an offer...'

'Well, even supposing I agreed, and could
get Ken to agree, we've no guarantee that
you'll be able to prove him innocent.'

'If I fail I don't get the title deeds. My
lawyer – Kyle Endicott – can hold them
until I've completed my side of the bargain.
That's fair enough, isn't it?'

'Could there be any plainer proof that
you're back of the place being burned
down?' Sally breathed. 'You offered before
to buy it, then Ken turned up and you were
prevented. Now you've worked out this new
scheme to get your own way. I thought it
was so you could get me. Now I realize it's
the Double G land, and all because you
know some secret which we don't.'

'Secret?' Billings looked puzzled, and it
seemed his bafflement was genuine. Then
he shrugged it away. 'That's the offer,' he
said. 'If you'll sell I'll go to work. Not
otherwise.'

Sally considered him in silent contempt
for a moment or two; then she sighed. 'All
right. I'll ride over to the jail and see what
Ken says, then I'll come back here.'

'You've no need. I'll ride over with you.'

And Clem Billings did so, though he and Sally exchanged no words during the journey. When they had reached the sheriff's office, Billings remained outside on his mare, waiting. Garson raised no objection to the girl having a brief talk with Ken in the small, strongly barred adobe jail at the back of the office.

'Why the devil should we?' Ken demanded, when she had given him the facts. 'It's simply playin' into his hands. It's plain that he's the one who's been up to all this double-crossin' an' now he's played a trump card.'

'Ken, you're in a dreadful spot,' Sally insisted, with quiet patience. 'I don't like the sell-out any more than you do – but we can't afford to take chances with your life even if that dirt-heap we own could be worth a million dollars a square foot. We've *got* to take any chance we can to free you. Once you *are* free maybe we can go a good deal further.'

Ken began arguing again, but with less resistance. At last the girl had broken him down completely. He could not escape the fact that his life was worth more than ranch land, no matter how valuable the secret hidden in it.

'OK,' he growled at length. 'I agree. You own the title deeds, of course, but after we got married my lawyer Mark Denning has them, over in Glover City. You say that Endicott's actin' for Billings? His office is not far down the street from here. Tell him to contact Denning and fix things up so you can sell the land, then he can hang on to the deed until we get some action. And no action, no transfer. Once I can get out of here,' he breathed, 'I'll deal with that skunk Clem Billings as I see fit! Maybe if I can prove his double-dealing, the transfer will be null and void. Yeah, that's it...'

Sally stayed with him a little longer, calming his impetuous temper; then she hurried to where Billings still sat on his mare. He listened in silence as she recounted what had happened.

'Good enough,' he assented. 'From now on I'm goin' to get busy on my own. The moment Ken is released he'll join you in the hotel – and that'll be the time when you hand over the deed. You go ahead and fix things through the lawyers.'

He said no more, raising his hat and then spurring his mount forward. He only went as far as the end of the main street, however, and there remained concealed, watching

Sally's movements.

At length he saw her leave Lawyer Endicott's office, the legal man at her side – and later still they both emerged from the sheriff's office, from where the girl had sent a telegraph message to Denning in Glover City. Then the girl went across the road to her hotel and Kyle Endicott returned to his own office.

Billings smiled grimly to himself, then rode his horse as far as the livery stable, left it there, and walked the short distance along the boardwalk to Ma Brayson's rooming house.

As he strode up on to the front porch he found fat old Ma Brayson sunning herself as she sprawled in a rocking-chair.

'Howdy, Ma,' he greeted, and she nodded with easy familiarity. 'You got a cattle-dealer stayin' with you? Checked in early this mornin', mebbe?'

'Sure have,' the old woman assented. 'Rare bird he is too. A real dude if ever I see'd one.'

'Is he in?'

'Yes. Said he wus a-goin' to ketch up on some sleep, an' I wus to see he weren't disturbed. An' that, Clem Billings, includes you!'

'Not this time,' Billings answered grimly. 'I've business with that gent. Where's his room? Come on, Ma – give! This is important. You know me. I never pulled anythin' on you yet.'

'Well, all right – room nineteen, top of th' stairs,' she sighed. 'I guess you could've slipped in without me knowin', eh?'

Billings grinned and strode into the hall, hurried up the staircase to the top. He found door 19 and knocked on it sharply. He expected a sleepy reply, but a quite wakeful voice snapped:

'Well, who is it?'

'Open up. I can't shout this information through a keyhole.'

There was a long pause, then the lock clicked and the door opened a little. The man on the other side was clean-shaven, neatly attired in spotless shirt and riding-pants, was largely made, black-haired and small-eyed. He held a .45 at the ready as Billings lunged in on him and shut the door.

'Well, what d'you want?' the man demanded.

'Just to look at you,' Billings responded, his keen eyes assessing every detail of the man's face and figure. Then he added drily, 'Kinda nervous for a cattle-dealer, aren't you? Expectin' unpleasant visitors?'

The man hesitated and then put his gun down on the dressing-table.

'I have enemies,' he admitted. 'Reckon most cattle-dealers have. Since you're not one of 'em it's all right.'

'You mean you hope I'm not,' Billings corrected grimly. 'You're the guy who saw the stage hold-up, aren't you? The one who handed a spiel about it to the sheriff?'

'Sure I did. I figured it was my duty.'

'Y'know,' Billings said, whirling up a chair and reversing it, so that he sat with his elbows on the back, 'I've bin thinkin'. There's a gunhawk came to this town recently by the name of Cal Reynolds. Quite a young chap, 'bout your build, but with a record so dirty that nobody'll employ him. Nobody decent, that is. One thing he can do is shoot a speck of dirt from a cayuse's tail without disturbin' a hair. As a rule Cal Reynolds has a scrub beard an' an old suit and hat. Any night y'can see him boozin' in the Blue Dollar, usin' up some money he's made owl-hootin' for some outfit. But if Cal Reynolds was to shave and dress himself natty, same as you are, he'd look just like you.'

The man glared. 'What the blue hell are

you talkin' about? I'm Brice Taytham, a cattle-dealer from Kansas.'

'Stop kiddin' yourself,' Billings answered coldly. 'No cattle-dealer worth anythin' would ride the trail solo by night an' on a horse. He'd do it by railroad or stage. *You're Cal Reynolds!* And the other night when Ken Bradmore and me got to fightin' you was among the watchers, lookin' as usual like a broken-down tramp. I remember it clearly. You were at the next table to where I was playin' poker, because I told Slim Halligan to go and sit with you.'

The man's small eyes strayed to his gun – then back to Billings' .38 as it rested significantly on the chair-back, pointing at him.

'So?' he demanded angrily.

'So you're goin' to start talkin',' Billings explained. 'When I heard about the hold-up I thought of a gunhawk of Ken Bradmore's build. I know most everybody around this district, and you just fitted. See?'

Billings jumped up suddenly and, disregarding his gun, he smashed his left fist into the man's jaw, sending him reeling against the bed end.

'*Give!*' he ordered, 'or I'll beat the hide off you! On the night you were in th' saloon, when Ken Bradmore and me were fightin', you switched his gun just as last night you framed that hold-up' on him, doin' it yourself and plantin' the gold in Tin Pan's cabin.'

'Like hell I did–'

The fist came again and whirled the gunhawk drunkenly against the dressing-table. He clutched at it desperately and for his revolver, but he never seized his gun. An uppercut rocked him from his feet and into the corner by the window.

'Well?' Billings demanded. 'Reckon it don't matter to me if I break your jaw or your neck. Start talkin'!'

'OK, OK, I framed it,' Reynolds panted. 'I swapped the guns an' framed the robbery–'

'On whose orders?' Billings interrupted. 'That's what I want to know! I ain't carryin' a torch for Ken Bradmore, but I want the facts because *I'm* gettin' plenty of suspicion myself.'

'I don't know whose orders–'

Billings reached out and hauled the man to his feet, slapping his palm savagely across his face.

'Don't hand me that, Reynolds! You must know who, else how could you follow out orders?'

'It's truth!' Reynolds snarled. 'All I know is six men came to my shack jus' before sundown on the night you and Bradmore fought. They told me they knew he'd probably be there and they gave me a Colt that I was to put in his left-hand holster, takin' his own gun. I had to figger my own way of doin' it – so I chose the time when you was fightin' with him.'

'Keep talkin',' Billings ordered.

'With them they brought a shirt and ridin'-pants an' hat, same colour as Bradmore's. After cleanin' myself up I was to wear 'em and hold up the night stage from Antelope, takin' the gold-bags and dumpin' 'em in the cabin. I was also to try and get Bradmore to follow me. If his wife followed too that didn't matter, just as long as he did. I managed that and got back to my shack OK.'

'And then?'

'Them six critters was waitin' for me. They took Bradmore's gun from me, showed me a dude outfit, which I've got on now, and th' horse they'd brought. They told me to doll myself up, ride that horse, and in the mornin' pretend to be a cattle-dealer and tell the sheriff that I'd seen the stage robbed and followed the outlaw to the cabin in the creek.

I had to tell the sheriff quick in case Bradmore noticed th' switch in guns. That weren't likely since the butts was the same and one doesn't look often at one's guns – an' left-hand ones hardly at all. I did as I was told and they paid me four hundred dollars for it. I did th' job 'cos they'd threatened to blast the daylights outa me if I didn't.'

'Then what in heck are you skulkin' around here for? Your job's done, isn't it?'

'They told me to stick around for a day or two so as to seem like a genuine witness – and then blow town. I could come back as Cal Reynolds any time I wanted.'

'An' you don't know who the men were?'

'So help me, no. They was kerchief-masked and I never heard their voices before. They said they knew me as an owl-hooter and had those jobs for me – so I did 'em, standin' to collect four hundred.'

'An' what about Tin Pan's shootin'? You do that?'

'No.' Reynolds shook his head emphatically. 'Never touched the old buzzard, an' I don't know who did.'

'Right now,' Billings said, lifting up his gun from the chair, 'that ain't important. You've got more talkin' to do – to the sheriff! Start movin'!'

Towards sundown that same evening Clem Billings rode in to the Treble Circle ranch, fastened his mare to the porch rail, and then mounted the steps to the screen door. Axia, the half-breed, narrow-faced male servant, admitted him.

'Miss Alland in?' Billings asked curtly, doing nothing to disguise his dislike of the man.

'In lounge, sir,' Axia responded, motioning to it. 'Do not think she expects you.'

Billings crossed the broad hall of the ranch house and entered the big comfortable lounge to find Beatrice Alland seated in the evening sunlight going through a sheaf of accounts.

'Hello, Clem.' She got up and extended her hand. 'What's on your mind?'

'Business – and pleasure,' he responded, smiling, and handed her a folded legal deed. Surprised, she straightened it out and read through it slowly.

'Well! So you finally managed it,' she murmured in her drowsy voice. 'Bought the land where the Double G stood – including the mine. How did this come about?'

'It's a long story. I had to spring Ken Bradmore from jail on a murder and hold-

176

up rap – but I managed it. My price for doin' it was his land, an' here it is, all signed, sealed, and settled. I own it now. As for Ken and his wife, they've gone back to some cabin in the creek, presumably while they think out where they'll go next.'

'I heard about the murder and hold-up charge,' the girl said pensively. 'How on earth did you manage to clear it up?'

'Oh, I just found out who really did it. There was a matter of switched guns and double identity – but I haven't found out who killed Tin Pan, an' I don't care if I never do. That gunhawk Cal Reynolds was the critter I wanted, and right now he's in jail. Seems he got his orders from six mystery outlaws... Anyway, there's nothin' now to stop us gettin' married, is there?'

'That,' Beatrice Alland said, as she tossed the deed on the table, 'depends.'

'On what?' Billings caught her roughly by the shoulders and forced her to look at him. 'Look here, Bee, let's get this straight! You said you'd marry me if I could buy the Double G, so that your ranch an' mine could absorb it and we'd have one big spread. Then when I failed to swing the deal the first time you refused to marry me–'

'Not because you failed to swing the deal,'

the girl interrupted. 'But because you were so attracted to Sally Bradmore! And I'm not so sure that you still aren't!'

'Darn it, Bee, do you think I'd have been to all this effort t' buy up the land – in the hopes it would cinch things between us – if I wanted Sally Bradmore? I'm not that crazy! Sure I like the gal – might even have gone further if Ken hadn't turned up, but that's all finished with. I've got the Double G land, an' our two ranches can absorb it, like we said. You an' me married will make us the most powerful owners in the whole valley – even the state, as time goes on. We c'n soon restore the Double G spread.'

The girl said nothing. She reflected for a while.

'What guarantee have I got that you still won't make a play for Sally Bradmore, husband or no husband?'

'You've a mighty good one, if you'd just stop to think about it!' he snapped. 'I *could* have let him swing for a crime he didn't commit, which would have left Sally free had I wanted her. Instead I chose to get the ranch land to seal things between you an' me – and freed Ken. What more d'you want?'

Beatrice Alland smiled faintly. 'Mmmm –

looked at that way I suppose it's logical. All right, Clem, I'll marry you, but don't go running away with the idea that it's for love. It's partly business.'

'From you I didn't expect much else,' he answered grimly. 'Just the same you're still a woman, and I'm still a man. Mebbe we'll get to thinkin' a lot more about that as time goes on.'

'Maybe,' she agreed casually, 'but I doubt it... Anyway, leaving aside the emotional issues, Clem – my agreeing to marry you carries a proviso.'

'Proviso!' Billings echoed in amazement. 'My God, why can't you act like a woman instead of the head of a prosperous ranch?'

'Listen to me, Clem.' The girl's voice was quiet but firm. 'I have all the responsibility of this place on my shoulders and I have to plan things so that everything I do contributes in some way to making my position secure. I'll marry you – yes, and even be the kind of wife you expect, but I must insist on a fifty-fifty partnership.'

'Well, naturally. What's mine is yours. That's marriage law anyway.'

'I know, but I want it on firmer ground than that. A wife can be gypped out of her possessions sometimes. I'm going to make a

Will, and so are you, to be drawn up and properly witnessed by Kyle Endicott, the lawyer, each of us leaving our entire possessions to the other in case an accident should happen. And they're not uncommon in this part of the world.'

Billings hesitated for only a moment, but he was looking a trifle puzzled. 'Well, okay, if that's how you want it. Good idea, in fact. It makes both of us safe.'

Beatrice Alland nodded. 'So I think. I'll send Axia into town to fetch Endicott back this evening and we'll both get married by licence and settle our Wills...'

She turned away, leaving Billings looking somewhat baffled by this matter-of-fact betrothal, and rang the bell. There was a pause and then the half-breed came in unsteadily, his small dark eyes bloodshot.

'The man's drunk!' Billings declared in disgust, staring at him.

'Yes!' Beatrice Alland's eyes narrowed at the man. 'Been at the bottle again, have you, Axia?' she snapped. 'Remember what I told you last time?'

'Little drink no harm,' the half-breed retorted sullenly, in his curious mixed-up English.

'Get out, you dirty little tramp, and sleep

it off!' the girl ordered. 'If you're ever drunk again whilst on my property I'll have the boys kick you off it – for good.'

Axia turned and lurched out, slamming the door. Billings gave the girl a glance.

'I'd better fetch the lawyer myself,' he said. 'And I don't know why you keep that shifty-eyed little horror on as a servant, Bee. You know as well as I do that he's a thief, and mebbe a murderer, too, for all we know.'

'It's *because* I know that he's a thief,' she answered calmly. 'He has to obey me – or else. Those without a record aren't too keen on working as servants... OK, Clem, you fetch Endicott. I'll be waiting when you get back.'

12

'Well, Sal, as far as I can see there's nothing for it now but to hit the trail and start again someplace else,' Ken Bradmore decided, as he and the girl sat on the cabin porch after supper that evening. 'I reckon Clem Billings did me a good turn by getting me out of jail, but he also did us both a bad one by buying up the remains of the Double G. Nothin' for us to do now but get out. I've given up th' idea of gettin' even with him.'

Sally contemplated the tall grey peaks against the salmon-tinted flood of sunset, and she sighed.

'Yes, I suppose you're right,' she agreed. 'And it's such a horrible shame! I'd planned so many things we were going to do in this wonderful stretch of country. Somewhere else, in a city for instance, it will just be a humdrum existence. No fighting for ourselves. And once we get city-stamped we'll never want to come back to this, Ken.'

He put an arm about her shoulder. 'I know, kid, an' it breaks my heart as much as it does yours – but we have to face facts.'

'I still don't like going without knowing what there is on that land of ours,' Sally insisted, 'and it seems to me that now Clem Billings has bought the land we've got a better chance than we ever had of finding out the truth. In spite of all he's done I think now, like you've always done, that he's back of everything – and now he has the land he can do as he likes with it. If we could only stay long enough we might discover what he's after. It won't do *us* any good to know, of course, but at least it would satisfy our curiosity. And it must be something important or Tin Pan wouldn't have been shot down so ruthlessly. And remember – we still don't know who killed him. After the way he helped you out of that fire don't you think we sort of owe it to his memory to find his killer?'

'Yeah that's true enough,' Ken admitted.

'We can go on living in this cabin here for at least another month: there are enough food supplies for that, and in any case we have the sale money in the bank now if we need to restock. What do you say if we do that, and in the meantime see what happens?'

'OK, but you mustn't forget that some-body is trying to dry-gulch us, and they'll doubtless go on tryin' as long as we stick around this neighbourhood.'

'I'll risk it – if you will.'

Ken grinned. 'What a question! All right then, we... Say,' he broke off in surprise, 'what's that?'

Sally followed the direction of his gaze and then gave a start. To their left, where the canyon trail curved and twisted down into the valley, a tall pillar of black smoke was rising into the sunset, its topmost driftings slashed with sullen amber light where the dying rays caught it.

'Fire somewhere down in the valley.' Ken scrambled to his feet. 'We'd better take a look. Pass the time on, anyway. Maybe the six terrorists have struck again, at one of the other two ranches.'

Sally nodded and rose beside him. To saddle their mounts did not take above a few moments; then they sped them down the trail as fast as they could go. Reaching the point where it curved and gave them a view of the valley they drew rein and leaned on their saddle horns, looking towards Beatrice Alland's Treble Circle. Certainly there was evidently a good deal wrong down there.

The ranch house itself was smoking furiously on one side with occasional glimpses of flame. Around it, working with ceaseless effort, were the men who comprised the ranch's outfit, obviously doing their utmost to quell the outbreak. The real activity, however, lay in the corrals where cattle, frightened by the fire's advance, were streaming away in their hundreds towards the pasture, pursued by punchers and, dimly visible was a black-coated figure, Clem Billings.

'Fire and stampede,' Ken muttered,

watching the scene. 'It looks like the same sort of thing that happened to me. It's goin' to be tough goin' for Miss Alland, too. Reckon I'd better give a hand with those cattle.'

'But why?' Sally asked blankly. 'What's it got to do with you?'

'Technically, nothin' – but there's an unwritten law that in a stampede you try an' help your neighbour if you can. She's my neighbour – or was. I'll see what I c'n do.'

He spurred his horse's flanks and started off at a swift canter into the valley. Sally followed him at top speed – not because she had any intention of joining in the struggle to save the steers, but because the thought of being left alone in the gathering dark scared her.

Down in the valley the fingers of the night were far extended, and the twilight was deepened by the clouds of smoke sweeping the heavens. Ken, ahead of the girl, gave a glance back and then lost sight of her in the smoke-wreaths as he plunged into the struggle to cut off the cattle's mad flight into the pastures. Trained rancher as he was he knew every move ahead of time.

For ten minutes he was busy with the stockwhip from his saddle and his Colt, firing it into the air; then in the gloom he came suddenly upon Billings. Billings gave him a surprised look and jolted his mare to a stop.

'Thanks for the help,' he panted, wiping his hand over his dirty, perspiring face. 'I think this herd'd have gotten outa control but for you helpin' on this side.'

'Just a neighbourly act,' Ken replied. 'I saw the smoke from up yonder. What happened, anyway? Terrorists strike like they did at me?'

'Nope. That blasted half-breed servant of Bee's got drunk and knocked over the oil-lamp in the kitchen. Which reminds me I'd better see how things are goin' at the ranch house.'

'Before you do,' Ken said, 'I reckon I ought to thank you for springin' me out of the hoosegow – even if it did have a tough price. Mebbe I've had you figgered wrong, Clem.'

'Sure you have,' Billings grinned. 'I've no grudge against you and never did have. Only thing I don't like you for is that you spotted Sally and married her before I did! As it is I married Bee Alland this evenin'…'

He rode off into the smoke and darkness, leaving Ken with his whip and gun. He turned back to his task and by degrees, aided by the other cowpunchers, the herd was forced slowly back towards the corrals. Then, as he found himself surrounded by several steers, Ken frowned hard. One of them had a broken horn, somehow familiar.

He dropped quickly from the saddle, stopped the beast's progress, and peered closely at the nearer foreleg in the gloom. Faintly visible was a badly erased 'G' within a 'G', his own brand mark when he had possessed a ranch and a herd of his own; and over it was a triple circle, branded deep. Then the steer had moved away, blatting uneasily as it floundered with the rest of the herd.

Grim-faced, Ken stood looking about him, watching steer after steer. Finally, satisfied that the stampede was in hand, he rode out of the smoke into pale grey darkness on the edge of the melee to where Sally was waiting for him on her restless pinto.

'All set?' she enquired. 'It looks like the fire's under control,' she added, nodding towards the ranch house, from which smoke had ceased to pour.

'Not quite all set, Sal,' Ken answered bitterly. 'I've a few questions to ask Miss Alland. Several of the steers in her corral are mine – rustled, with their brands not too well changed. I'll be back in a moment.'

He rode as far as the ranch house, pulled open the screen-door, and strode across the hall into the lounge. He was just in time to see Beatrice Billings, her face coldly venomous in the light of the oil-lamp, delivering a murderous whiplash across the back of her half-breed servant.

'*Now get out!*' she spat at him, flinging the stockwhip on the table. 'And don't ever come back or I'll flay the rest of your hide off you!'

The man scuttled towards the door, a stooped, sinister-looking creature.

'Me kill you one day,' he whispered fiercely, looking back. 'You see!' Then he blundered past Ken and out on to the porch.

The girl rancher gave a grim smile and glanced towards Billings, her new husband standing near the fireplace; then her eyes caught sight of Ken as he lounged forward.

'Don't spare the lash much do you, Miss Alland?' he asked grimly.

'It's *Mrs Billings* now,' she answered briefly. 'And as for my lashing Axia, I'd damned good reason to. He set fire to my place through drinking in defiance of my orders. Scum like him need teaching a lesson.'

Ken said nothing for a moment. In the heat of the moment he had forgotten all about the girl's marriage.

'The trouble is that you *can't* teach his breed,' Billings said. 'They're vicious, cunnin' as snakes... You'd better watch out for him, Bee, or he'll get you one day. Don't forget how he threatened you.'

The girl gave him a glance of scorn and then turned to Ken.

'Well, Mr Bradmore, Clem tells me you've been lending a hand in saving my cattle? That was real decent of you.'

'Oh, that's OK, Miss – I mean Mrs Billings. Only ... they don't all happen to be your cattle.'

'They ... what?' The girl stared at him. 'What do you mean?'

'I'm thinkin',' Ken said quietly, 'that I'm entitled to some sort of explanation. Several of the steers I handled are mine; they must have disappeared when my ranch was burned down and I was attacked. My brand has been half-obliterated and yours burned in over the top.'

'That's ridiculous!' Billings snapped angrily, and Ken glanced at him.

'Don't take my say-so, Clem. Go take a look for yourself.'

'We all will,' the girl decided, and led the way out of the room.

Amidst the string of oil-lamps which had been lighted around the corral she led an investigation of the steers, her face becoming more perplexed and Billings' more grim at the indisputable evidence. Finally, the foreman was called and Ken stood waiting, out of earshot. At length the girl and Billings came back to him.

'There's only one explanation for this, Mr Bradmore,' the girl said. 'That low-down thief of a half-breed must have done it. He used to do a lot of horse-stealing at one time: I've full evidence of it. He has a particular hatred of ranchers, and evidently you were on his list. I gather it must have been he who burned down your ranch and attacked you.'

'Uh-huh,' Ken acknowledged slowly. 'And men to help him? Tin Pan said he saw half a dozen.'

'I don't think Axia would have found it hard to get men to help him. There are always outlaws riding the range. My guess is that Axia ran the steers in with my herd, trusting that the great numbers of them compared to your few wouldn't be noticed by my foreman – but in case they were he amateurishly changed the brands. Later on he probably intended to run them out some place where he could sell them.'

'Yeah, could be,' Ken admitted. 'Fact remains that they're my property.'

'You can't do anythin' with them when you've no ranch,' Billings pointed out. 'Best thing you can do is name a price for them an' square things off. I counted about fifty head.'

'There were seventy in my corral,' Ken responded. 'As for payment, I'm not takin' any.'

'But you must!' the girl insisted.

'Nope! That would make 'em your property and destroy my own hold on them. I'm still callin' them my property, and first thing in the morning I'm going to ask the sheriff what should be done about them. Cattle stealin' is a mighty big offence. That servant you kicked out has got to be found and made to speak – explain exactly what he did.'

Ken turned on his heel without another word and left Beatrice Billings and the rancher staring after him blankly.

'I have the idea,' Billings said at length,

191

'that he thinks one of *us* is responsible for that rustling an' the firing of his ranch.'

The girl reflected. 'Yes and that being so our best move is to get Axia back. I happen to know that he's got a hideout up in the mountains. I think we should go and fetch him ourselves – never mind waiting for the sheriff to do it – and force him to speak. Since it's dark we can probably take him by surprise.'

'OK,' Billings agreed. 'I'll get the horses.'

Soon he and the girl were mounted and speeding across the valley, the girl leading the way. Billings asked no questions, but he was inwardly surprised at the devious route she took, each mile carrying them further into the rocky wilderness with its forgotten and half-buried trails. When they had been on the move for nearly an hour and were deep in the mountain country Billings drew to a halt.

'Just a minute, Bee, what *is* this?' he demanded. 'How can you be sure Axia is up here?'

The girl drew up her horse quickly, so she and Billings were side by side on the mountain trail, the rearing escarpments to one side of them and a 400-feet drop into a gorge on the other.

'I can't,' she answered, and Billings could dimly see her face in the starlight. 'In fact, I don't even know if he is. I don't care, either.'

'Then what—'

'You have the suspicion, Clem, that I took those cattle and burned down that ranch of Ken Bradmore's. I've seen it in your face ever since we examined those steers with the changed brands.'

'Can't blame me for being suspicious,' he said, 'only I reckon I must be dead wrong—'

'No, you're right,' the girl interrupted calmly. 'I *did* have cattle taken and the Double G burned down. I thought Ken Bradmore would burn with it, only things went wrong for me through Tin Pan interfering. Then I did my best to get you to buy the property, offering to marry you if you did. Finally you did get it, and I married you as a business proposition.'

Billings waited, the light too dim to show his expression, but the girl did hear his little intake of breath.

'I saw Tin Pan kidnap Sally,' the girl continued. 'My ranch is within seeing distance of the ruined Double G, remember. I followed them at a safe distance as far as the cabin. By listening outside the slightly opened window of the bedroom I heard Tin

Pan say that he knew of something valuable on the Double G land and could take Ken and Sally Bradmore straight to it. He tried to, but I shot him before he could manage it. It wasn't so hard for me. I learned to handle a gun when I was a youngster. I tried to get Bradmore too, but missed because his horse reared at the wrong time.'

'But – what *is* this something that's so valuable?' Billings demanded.

'That's my business,' the girl's cold voice responded. 'All I will tell you is that there's something valuable buried deep in it, which I can only get at by drilling the land. I couldn't do that without owning it, and I didn't want to advertise myself as a buyer, so I had you do it. Fortunately you met Mrs Bradmore early on and started the ball rolling.'

'It doesn't seem to me that Tin Pan had any need of drillin' if he was taking the Bradmores straight to the spot,' Billings snapped.

'Obviously Tin Pan knew a secret way to get at this buried treasure,' the girl said. 'And you can call it that. I'd have dearly loved to know the way, but that would have meant that the Bradmores would have known, too, so I shot Tin Pan down. Since then I have tried to find the trail that Tin Pan was intending to take, but I haven't managed it. Now it doesn't matter. Since I own the Double G land I can start drilling and locate the treasure that way instead.'

'Drilling?' Billings repeated. 'Then you mean it's oil?'

'No. It isn't oil. By "drilling" I mean digging down, if you want to split hairs.' Silence, and the dim starlight. Then Billings spoke again.

'Then you burned down that ranch and tried to kill Ken Bradmore...'

'I did, because there was no other way of making him go. I knew his wife was coming and I couldn't see that she would prove such a tough person to buy the land from with him gone. Only, as I say, things went wrong. Tin Pan gummed up everything, even to letting Ken and Sal know that the land is valuable. I'd hoped, when I framed Ken for murder and outlawry, that he'd be hanged, again leaving only his wife to deal with, but you with your stupid blundering got him free, to remain as a danger. However, since you also bought the land I suppose that much stands in your favour.'

'What kind of a woman have I married?' Billings whispered. 'I admit I wondered at the speed with which our union was made legal, but-'

'Frankly, Clem, I've no further use for you or I wouldn't have told you this much,' Beatrice said coldly. 'If the sheriff is called in about the cattle – and apparently Bradmore means business – your very looks would give me away. I don't propose to risk it. I had you make over the land to me, by your Will, for only one reason – to claim it. My making things over to you in return was so much moonshine... Everything clear now? Naturally, I have six gunhawks working for me, the six Tin Pan saw. Also, if you remember, it was I who incited you into fighting Ken – or rather I incited *him* into fighting you – in the Blue Dollar that night.'

Suddenly, before the dumbfounded Billings had a chance to think what to do next, the girl's vicious small-tailed horsewhip slashed out and struck his mare a savage cut across the withers. She shied and whinnied in anguish, wheeled round, and missing her footing on the narrow pathway, slid helplessly over its edge. Billings gave one desperate, despairing scream as he and the animal tumbled outwards into space and vanished in the abyss cloaked in night below.

Slowly the girl replaced the whip in the

saddle and sat thinking.

'Ken Bradmore said "in the morning",' she mused. 'But a lot can happen before morning which can stop him speaking – ever. Yes! Yes, indeed!'

Her mind made up, she edged her sorrel away from the danger spot and kept on riding until she struck a narrow trail leading to the mountain heights. It was half an hour's tough ascent, but it finally brought her to an area where tall spurs of rock, delicately balanced by natural forces, stabbed their points into the night sky. Amidst them she paused, looking down the vast slope in the rising moonlight.

In the bottom of the canyon created by the slope was a solitary cabin, seeming microscopic and hardly visible in the pale light – but it was enough to satisfy the girl. She peered at her watch and found it was just on midnight.

She waited for another hour just to make sure that Ken and Sally would probably be asleep, then taking a lariat from the saddle horn, she fastened it round one of the lower spurs of balanced rock and carried the rope back to the saddle.

Remounting, she opened a sharp jackknife and urged the sorrel forward, watching over her shoulder.

Three times the powerful animal had to tug before the lowest rock was jolted sideways out of position. Instantly the girl slashed the rope through and spurred the horse forward. Then she drew rein and watched. The slipping of the lowest rock released the balance of the giants surrounding it.

In a gathering thunder they began rolling, down towards the cabin in the canyon below.

13

'What in blazes is the matter with those cayuses?' Ken growled impatiently, sitting up in the crude bed and staring towards the moonlit window of the cabin.

'They're obviously restive over something,' Sally responded drowsily, lying at his side.

'Mebbe a prowler. I'm goin' to take a look, and quieten the beasts down if I can.'

He scrambled out of the bed, a rather odd-looking figure in the dim light, since he was wearing one of the nightshirts Tin Pan had possessed. Quickly he pulled on his riding-pants and half-boots and then went out to investigate. In the crude little stable at the side of the cabin the pinto and horse were both moving uneasily and whinnying at intervals.

'What goes on?' Ken demanded of them. 'Storm blown' up, or somethin'? Nothin' else as a rule starts y'going...'

He paused, frowning to himself. There was something queer in the air – a deep, satanic rumbling disturbing the peace of the night. Suddenly he thought he knew the reason for the animals' uneasiness. An earthquake perhaps...

The sound grew. He hurried out of the stable and looked about him in bewilderment; then his ear caught the direction of the growing sound, far up the mountain slopes. The rumbling changed to a gathering thunder and, in one petrified second, he realized what was coming.

He dashed back in the stable, released both animals and delivered a slap on their withers that sent them scampering; then he dived for the cabin and hurtled into the bedroom. Without a word to the half-sleeping Sally he whirled her up in his arms, together with the single blanket and blundered with her, protesting feebly, out of the cabin.

There was no time for anything but to run as he had never run before. And he did, putting down the astonished girl and telling her to run with him. Convinced by his tremendous urgency and scared by the gathering din she did not ask questions: she ran with him, submitting to being dragged, pulled and pushed, as he floundered amidst rocks, struggling as far away as possible from the centre of the valley floor.

Then behind them all hell broke loose. Gigantic boulders, visible in the moonrise, crashed down, followed by a hail of smaller rocks, clouds of dust and deluges of chippings. Before the thundering, roaring tide of earth the cabin, corral and stable completely vanished, and the avalanche swept on, raging along the canyon floor, until at last its fury was exhausted and only blinding clouds of dust remained, drifting on the night breeze.

'What – what happened?' Sally whispered, shaken to the core of her being, dragging the solitary blanket about her lightly-clad body.

'Evidently a rock fall.' Ken's voice was harsh. 'An avalanche – mebbe natural, mebbe not.'

'But nobody could *start* an avalanche, could they?'

'Given naturally balanced rocks they could, and there's plenty of 'em in these mountains. Seems to me, Sal, it was more than a coincidence that our cabin happened to be right in the line of fire.' Ken drew the back of his hand over his perspiring face. 'Thank God those two cayuses sensed what was comin'.'

'You set them free? Was there time?'

'Yeah just! But I reckon we'll never find 'em. Now, let's see what damage there is...'

They returned to the mountainous pile of stones and for the next half-hour busied themselves with moving the boulders to one side. Cabin and stables were completely buried. It was more by chance than anything else that they came upon Sally's suitcase, battered and dented, but still with her belongings inside.

'Well, thank heaven for small mercies,' she commented. 'At least I can dress properly.'

She did so in the moonlight, whilst Ken stood looking about him.

'Well, that's the end of that,' he said at last. 'And of our cabin. An' the more I think of it the more sure I am it was a real effort to wipe us out – which makes me all the more determined to find out what goes on ... if you are?'

'Of course! More so than ever, in fact. Seems to me we've a better chance now of watching things and lying low. If the avalanche *was* deliberately planned we can be sure the planner thinks we died in it. He'd never guess the horses saved us. And that means,' Sally added, 'that we'll be thought dead.'

'Yeah.' Ken rubbed his chin and reflected. 'We can get shelter in one of the mountain caves: there are dozens of 'em around, and we can feed on what we can get. I've got my guns, and there's birds an' animals to kill for food. Point is, we can stick around until we do see what's on our land.'

'Uh-huh – only it will mean you can't go and tell the sheriff about those stolen steers of yours. You'd be seen.'

'I'm more interested in seein' what's on our land. The steers can wait ... an' I wish I didn't have to believe what keeps drummin' in my mind.'

'What's that?'

'That Clem's new wife is responsible for stealin' those steers o' mine. I can't think that that half-breed would do it and put the cattle amongst hers: doesn't make sense to my way of thinkin'. And I'm durned sure that Clem Billings, had he taken 'em, would have put 'em amongst his own on the Flying S ... so that only leaves Miss Alland – I mean Mrs Billings – for it.'

'But you can't mean that *she*–'

'That's the way it looks; but what we want is proof. If we can only catch her, or whoever is back of all this, up to some dirty work on our land we can come into the open. Right now let's find ourselves a cave and try an' finish off some of the sleep we've missed.'

This was a task that took them nearly two hours of wandering in the moonlight, by which time they were both too exhausted to talk any further. They crept into the warm dryness of the cave, settled themselves on the floor, and slept, using the girl's suitcase and some of its contents as a pillow, and the blanket Ken had snatched her in.

When they awoke it was dawn. For a time they sat looking at each other and then the girl gave a faint smile.

'You look quite picturesque in a nightshirt and riding pants,' she commented drily. 'Quite original!'

Ken felt his unshaven chin, looked down at himself, then grinned.

'You'd better get used to seein' this outfit, Sal, because I can't change it until I come back from the dead. Pity I hadn't spare clothes in that suitcase of yours. Anyway, I've got to start lookin' around for something to eat. Looks as if we'll have to be content with water to drink for some time to come. Here,' he handed over one of his guns, 'take this to protect yourself with while I'm gone. I don't expect trouble, but you never know.'

She nodded and he emerged from the cave into the cool of the morning, moving slowly amidst the rocks and occasional outcroppings of juniper trees. He had no particular idea what kind of food he was looking for – something in the way of a small animal, a squirrel perhaps, which could be cooked over a well-concealed camp-fire. Or maybe a bird of some kind if he could kill it with a stone's throw. The last thing he wanted to do was use his gun.

Several times he came across a resting flock of Sonora pigeons and picked up a piece of rock to take aim – but he was unlucky. The potential 'breakfast' took to the air and was gone with shrill, indignant cries.

Disgusted, Ken went on again, following

an old, tangled trail long since abandoned – and suddenly two ground-squirrels caught his eye.

He moved cautiously again, took a few paces, and then to his alarm the earth gave way beneath him. He went crashing through a rough tangle of branches and vines, down some twenty feet into the ground, crashing into a kind of pit. He was bruised, but the branches had broken his fall somewhat. He staggered to his feet and peered about him in the dim light.

He was in a deep, circular well, apparently natural, blown out of the rocks, but the top through which he had fallen had plainly been disguised by human hands. The thought of a mantrap occurred to him, and then he shook his head. Hardly that. More likely an attempt to hide the spot. Hide the spot! He twirled round, new thoughts chasing through his mind. On three sides of him was the rock wall, but on the fourth there was a gaping hole, the entrance to a tunnel. He struck one of his few valuable matches and peered into it. The feeble light failed to penetrate above a few feet into total darkness.

'I wonder...' he breathed.

He debated for a moment, remembered

that Sally was waiting for him, and then made up his mind. With some difficulty he fought his way back up the sloping side of the pit to the disused trail again; then he looked about him. He could not be sure, but as he retraced his steps and looked at various rocks there was something familiar about it all – particularly one rock with a distinctive jutting top that he had seen by starlight.

'No doubt about it,' he muttered eventually, 'it's the trail Tin Pan was takin' us to that night when he was shot down, an' it looks like I've hit the very spot to which he was goin'...'

He halted, a flock of Sonora pigeons right ahead of him. Aching for a meal and feeling reckless after his discovery, he forsook caution, took careful aim and fired with the result that he arrived back at the cave with two dead pigeons for breakfast.

He prepared them for a crude roasting whilst Sally threw away the contents of a powder-tin, swilled it out at a nearby freshet, and used it to carry water. Over the not too successful meal, Ken told her of his experience.

'It's it!' she insisted, when he had finished. 'I don't see how it could be anything else.

That must have been where Tin Pan had intended taking us – and to hide the spot he'd covered it up with branches and things...' She pushed the remains of the meal on one side and scrambled to her feet. 'Come on: let's see what there is there. The sooner we know the sooner we can come out into the open and behave like normal human beings.'

Ken nodded and walked out after her on to the old trail. Knowing the way so intimately this time it did not take him long to bring her to the pit. He helped her down its shelving side, and together they stood peering at the tunnel mouth.

'I only hope I've enough matches to last out,' Ken said. 'Anyway, here goes...' His gun in one hand and a match in the other, Sally also with a gun cocked in readiness, he led the way into the darkness. When he had struck five matches without nearing any end to the tunnel he decided to conserve them and instead he and the girl progressed by feeling their way.

'From the roughness of these walls,' came Ken's voice, 'this is a natural mountain tunnel. Nothin' odd about that: dozens of 'em in these mountains. And it goes *down* all the time. Noticed?'

'Uh-huh – and judging from the angle of the sun when we dropped down in the pit we're moving due north, or in other words in the same direction as the Double G and our Grey Rock mine workings. It can't be more than two miles away from the mountains, and I should think we've covered that distance already.'

'Must be about that,' Ken agreed, but they continued advancing.

From the increasing staleness of the air as they went further they judged that the tunnel did not have a second outlet, otherwise there would have been a draught blowing through it.

'Seems to me...' Ken started to say; then he broke off as his voice echoed loudly. 'Hello! We're out of the tunnel and in a cave or something. Let's take a look.'

He risked another of his precious matches and before the glow had dimmed and expired he and Sally had had the chance to see that they were in a big natural cave, in the corner of which was stacked what looked to be small crates. They went over to them and Ken struck another match. Behind the crates was another tunnel entrance, which had been blocked by a fall of rock.

'Wells Fargo!' Sally cried, pointing to the faded painted words on the sides of the cases. 'Why, that was one of the old-time stage lines, wasn't it?'

'How right you are!' Ken breathed. He struck another match, tugged his knife from his hip-pocket, then set about the job of prising up the lid of the topmost case. The boarding, rotten with age, easily broke away. Astounded, he and the girl stared at dull yellow blocks faintly glinting.

'Gold!' Sally gasped. 'Gold ingots!'

'This all begins to make sense at last,' Ken said, his voice tense. 'In all these cases there must be thousands of dollars' worth of gold. Evidently at some time it was hijacked from the Wells Fargo stage and hidden here – but whoever did it never had the chance to claim it. Somebody else, in our day, got to know of it and moved heaven and earth to get the land under which it was buried – evidently not knowing the tunnel route leading to it. I'll gamble right now that we're under our own land, and right next to our mine workings...' He broke off as the match expired and there was total darkness.

He lit another match, and they both moved forward to look more closely at the stacked cases. Eventually the match expired and there was total darkness once more. At the same moment Sally gave a little cry of fright.

'Ken! I saw – I thought I saw something...'

Ken moved towards her in the darkness, and to his surprise she was trembling. He lit another match.

'On the floor, in amongst that pile of rocks in the far corner,' Sally whispered.

The flickering light revealed a skeletal hand protruding from the rocks.

'Hold this match, Sal,' Ken said, passing it to her, and dived forward. He began heaving the rocks aside, and continued for a short while after the match expired. Then he stepped back and lit another.

There were two skeletons partially revealed, still in rotted clothing.

'These must have been the original thieves,' Ken murmured. 'They've been buried here for years under a rockfall...'

Sally had overcome her initial fearful surprise. 'Maybe they fell out and one shot at the other?' she suggested. 'The firing could have brought the rock down on them...'

Ken grinned. 'Quite the detective, Sal, and who knows but what you could be right. And since dead men can't tell no tales, Tin

Pan was the only one who knew about this place,' he added, 'but, like he said, he wasn't interested since it was under our land.'

Sally gave a little shudder. 'Let's get out of here and tell the sheriff...'

She did not have the chance to finish her sentence. From the mountain tunnel along which they had come blasted the sudden concussion of a distant explosion. They waited, unable to grasp what had happened. Then suddenly they went reeling back as hot air slammed into them with the acrid fumes of gunpowder and they were hurled from their feet in the darkness, the match jerking from Ken's fingers and extinguishing itself.

'What the devil!' Ken gasped, scrambling up. 'You all right, Sal?'

'Yes... Yes, I'm all right.' As Ken struck another match she became visible, holding her shoulder painfully. 'I'm only a bit bruised. What do you suppose that was?'

'The worst, I'm afraid. I'll soon find out. Stay here: I can move quicker on my own.' Ken hurried out of the cave, leaving the girl in the dark. Since he knew it to be more or less straight, he was able to risk moving along the tunnel at a stumbling run, striking a match only at intervals.

Sally waited anxiously for what seemed an interminable interval, then gave a sigh of relief as he came back, striking a match. Its wavering light fell on his sombre face.

'That does it!' he declared. 'Somebody's blown up the tunnel so we can't get out again! And they've done it thoroughly! There must be numberless tons of rock in the way. We'd never get through it.'

The match expired slowly. Sally's voice was unsteady.

'Ken ... you mean...'

'Don't quite know what I mean, kid.' His arm stole about her shoulders. 'But the position certainly isn't rosy. I'm to blame for it, too,' he added bitterly.

'Why, what did *you* do?'

'Used my gun to get us some breakfast. I shouldn't have been such a damned fool. Somebody must have heard the shot an' investigated. Evidently we were followed down here. They set a fuse on some dynamite or blastin' powder behind us, to give themselves time to get clear, then...'

'What it really means is that – we're entombed?' Sally whispered. 'Buried alive?'

14

Ken did not answer. There was a long pause, then Sally's shaky voice said:

'Ken, I'm scared! I'd sooner have anything than this. Shut down here in the dark with those skeletons, just to – to die. I'd sooner have a bullet in the back any time, out in the open...'

'Take it easy,' he muttered. 'If the worst comes to the worst, we've both got loaded guns. We can take care of things that way. I suppose the idea is for us to pass out and then, after a reasonable time, whoever it is will come and get the gold and leave our bodies sealed here. Since the cabin was destroyed in that avalanche everybody will assume that was where we died. Come to think of it, it's pretty smart schemin'.'

He did not strike another match because he did not want to see the hopeless look on Sally's face.

'At least we c'n sit down,' he said, taking her arm.

They felt their way around to the cases of

gold and settled with their backs to them –
and the two skeletons. Ken put his invisible
gun on his upthrust knees, only ... only it
was not *entirely* invisible. He only realized
the fact after a moment or two.

'That's odd,' he murmured, puzzled.

'What is?' asked Sally's listless voice.

'This gun. I can see the barrel shining!
How's that come about when we're sealed
in?' He turned sharply, looking around and
above him.

'For cryin' out loud!' he exclaimed,
clutching the girl's arm. 'Take a look up
there!'

She gazed and gave a cry of delight. High
up, there was a thin hairline of brilliant light
– evidently the sky – shining in the dark.

'It's a fissure!' Ken said urgently. 'It wasn't
there before, either. That explosion must
have cracked the rocks. Point is, how can we
make it wider?'

'Use your gun! Fire at it!'

'An' let somebody above hear me? Might
even cause another cave-in. Have you forgotten what happened to our two friends
back there?' he added drily. 'Nope; we need
to think of somethin' better 'n that.'

He was stymied for a while; then Sally
gave a little cry.

'The gold! If we can get high enough and use a block each to bang away at the rock it shouldn't make too much noise – and we'll get better results than just using our gun barrels, even granting they'd stand up to such punishment.'

'You've got it!' Ken declared. 'Give me a hand.'

He turned to the cases, just faintly visible in the crack of light now that their eyes had accustomed themselves. For half an hour they moved the heavy cases about until they had them poised none too securely in a stepped tower, and with the possibility that the wood might give way.

'I'll go first,' Ken said, and climbed cautiously to the top. Since nothing alarming happened, he helped Sally up to his side.

Without further words they each took a gold block from the topmost case and, using the heavy weight with piledriver effect, began chipping away at the underside of the thin fissure.

It was slow, gruelling work, with their arms held over their heads whilst they struggled – but they kept at it doggedly. Very slowly – so slowly that at times they wondered if they were making any progress at all – they made the fissure wider. But before it was big enough to permit of Ken's body passing through, the late evening had died into night and both were nearly too stiff to move. They realized they had been at their task for nearly eleven hours, able only to work at intervals before needing to rest.

'I think we can risk it now,' Ken said, as Sally half lay on the topmost case, massaging her aching shoulders. 'Good job it's gotten dark. Here I go!'

He poised, measured his distance to the grey hole, and then leapt. He gasped at the wrench on his aching arms as he gripped the edge of the gap as he passed it, and was forced to drag himself up by a sheer, convulsive muscular effort. Breathing hard, he pulled himself out on to the blackened ground and half lay for a moment, looking about him.

He had come out not far from the partly boarded-up entrance to their Grey Rock Mine, and further away he could dimly make out the ruins of the barn in their own fire-blasted Double G. The peace of the night was about him and apparently nobody was guarding the area. In the distance were the oil-lamp lighted windows of Beatrice Billings' ranch house – but in the opposite direction Billings' own Flying S was dark and seemed untenanted.

Ken stirred and peered down into the hole. 'All safe,' he whispered. 'Up you come, kid.'

'I haven't enough strength left in my arms,' Sally responded wearily from below.

Ken reached down with his arms. 'Grab,' he ordered. 'I'll pull you.'

Her hands gripped his elbows and he jerked himself upwards until she could transfer her grip to the edges of the hole. Reaching down again, he caught her under the arms and heaved backwards. Gasping, she came over the rim and fell on top of him.

'Done it,' he muttered, helping her up. 'You see where we are?'

She looked about her. 'Why, that's the mine entrance over there ... our own spread! That proves it! That stuff *is* under our land. What now then? Go for the sheriff?'

'It's a long way, tired as we are and without horses. I'm more inclined to tackle Mrs Billings at gunpoint and try and get some information out of her. I'm pretty sure by now that she's the cause of all our troubles. If she isn't I'll be able to judge quickly enough; 'sides, I don't quite understand why Clem Billings' ranch isn't lighted up. Even if he and Beatrice *are* married you'd think that he'd have his own ranch-work to get done, or that he'd have instructed someone to carry it out for him.'

'We'll both tackle her,' Sally decided, a surprising grimness in her tone, and recovering something of her strength now she was outside in the fresh air. 'I've one gun and you've the other.'

Side by side they moved silently through the darkness. Somewhat to their surprise there was no guard over the Treble Circle, though there were sounds of singing and laughter from the nearby bunkhouse.

'Must be pretty sure we can't make trouble,' Ken murmured, as he and Sally climbed over the yard's fence. 'All the better. Follow me.'

Still moving like shadows, they worked their way round to the front porch; then abandoning all caution, Ken put his heavy boot through the screen door and unlocked it from the inside. The main door was already open. With Sally beside him, he strode into the living-room. Beatrice Billings, who had heard them coming, stared in amazement as she sat in the lamplight, writing.

'Surprised?' Ken asked coldly, his gun

cocked. He glanced round for, and failed to see, Clem Billings.

'What do you want?' the girl asked, making a supreme effort at control and striving to sound casual.

'What do you think!' Ken snapped, and came forward to the table with Sally by his side. 'I've good reason for thinkin' that the person behind all my troubles – an' my wife's – is you! Those stolen steers of mine just can't be explained away by anybody *but* you!'

'Don't talk like a fool,' the woman retorted, rising. 'And by what right do you dare burst in here with such an accusation? Don't you realize,' she motioned to her black dress, 'that I'm in mourning? Can't you give me a bit of peace?'

'In mourning for whom?' Sally demanded.

'My husband.' The woman kept her voice low. 'He died last night. We were out riding the mountain trail and his horse took fright and bolted – into a chasm. The sheriff's boys recovered his body this afternoon, and the funeral's tomorrow.'

'So Clem's dead, is he?' Ken's face was harsh. 'Thanks for the information. That sort of makes things clearer than ever. A good horseman like Clem would never take a dive over a cliff. I'm suggestin' that it was deliberate murder! Why? Because it leaves you in possession of my ranch. I'll gamble that you've gotten it fixed all nice an' pretty to inherit it.'

The girl breathed hard. 'Will you get out of here?' she demanded.

'Not till you've started talkin',' Ken replied. 'Who killed Tin Pan? Who's bin tryin' to kill my wife an' me all this time?'

'Probably Axia, the half-breed,' Beatrice Billings retorted – then she recoiled with a gasp as Sally slapped her fiercely across the face. Ken gazed at Sally in surprise.

'Don't try that sort of game with me, Mrs Billings!' Sally warned. 'My husband may be pulling his punches because you're a woman – but I'm not going to. Come on – talk!'

'I'll see you in–'

'No you won't,' Sally interrupted, delivering another stinging blow. 'You'll talk, because if you don't...'

'Well? If I don't...?' the woman asked sourly.

'This!' From the box on the table Sally picked up a cigarette and lighted it. She coughed over it, only drew at it long enough to get it glowing, then she looked at the woman's face pensively.

'You just try burning me,' Beatrice Billings breathed, clenching her fists. 'Why, I'll give you such a–'

'No you won't,' Ken said, levelling his gun; 'unless you want a bullet in your leg. We mean business, Mrs Billings.'

'Right!' Sally confirmed venomously. 'I've hated you since the day we first met, when you looked at me as though I'd crawled out of the ground. You've tried to kill my husband and destroy our life together... By God, but I've had enough of you! It'll be real pleasure to make you smart...'

Beatrice Billings gasped as the cigarette's hot tip bit momentarily into her cheek and then withdrew. She swung out a swift, retaliatory blow, but missed completely. Then she caught sight of Ken's gun and calmed a little.

'All right,' she said, breathing heavily, her face contorted in pain. She fought for control, then, after a glance at the clock on the mantel, seemed to come to a decision. 'It's two to one, and I'm unarmed. I'll tell you. I've planned everything. I've men working for me. This morning one of them heard your gun and he traced you. Then he told me. I had the tunnel blown up. I can't think how you escaped.'

'You kill Tin Pan?' Ken demanded.

'Yes – but you can't prove it, any more than you can prove the admissions I'm making now...'

But by degrees the angry woman's story came out, expanding on the partial story as she had told it to the late Clem Billings.

'After he was widowed, my grandfather became an outlaw, and he was the man who stole that gold and hid it underground. But he'd been shot, and died before he could go back and reclaim it. He'd told only one person the secret of its location – his brother, Carl Wilcot...'

'Wilcot!' Ken exclaimed. 'You mean–'

'Carl Wilcot, who was also a widower then, was Boyd Wilcot's father. Ah, I see I've got your interest.' The woman smiled coldly, then continued, as Ken and Sally exchanged glances.

'Grandpa's injuries didn't kill him at first, but did incapacitate him. He'd hidden the gold in the mountains, caching it under-ground.' Again that grim smile. 'He'd had help with the heist, naturally, but his two partners never made it back out of that tunnel. The whole lot of something is much better than a third, don't you think?'

Sally gave a little shudder as she recalled the two skeletons they had found.

'But the law was catching up with him,' Beatrice Billings resumed her story. 'He was spotted as he left the mountain foothills. He was shot making his escape, but managed to get to Glover City and hole up there. While he was in hiding, he managed to get a letter sent to his brother, telling him about the gold. Incidentally, Grandpa Wilcot also had a daughter, who became my mother. She married my father and her name was changed to Alland...'

Ken gave a sideways glance at Sally, who was looking dumbfounded. 'Now things are beginning to make sense!' he observed. He turned to meet Beatrice Billings' mocking gaze. 'So your mother and Boyd Wilcot were cousins?'

'Yes. My parents died some years ago and Boyd Wilcot was my only living relative — until you got him hanged!' The woman was clearly enjoying the effect her revelations were having on her listeners. But there was more to come.

'Boyd Wilcot's father was strait laced, and refused to help his brother recover the gold. He ignored the letter, and its plea to get medical assistance to his brother. My grandpa died from his injuries, and, it seemed, his secret had died with him. Carl Wilcot told nobody about the letter, not the law, and not even his own son, who was by then living away from home anyway ... in 'Frisco. Evidently Carl was too ashamed of his brother to want anyone to know he was associated with an outlaw...'

'When I first met Wilcot, he told me that he had inherited his ranch from his father twenty years ago, and was already independently wealthy,' Ken said, frowning as he struggled to recall the conversation from a year earlier, when he had ridden with Wilcot to visit Sally's father at the Straight H.

'But later at the mine,' Ken resumed, 'he told us he'd gambled it away and was in debt to Jack Andrews. He killed Andrews and hid his body in old man Farraday's mine–'

'I still don't understand any of this!' Sally broke in fiercely. 'Why did Wilcot try to buy Dad's worthless mine? How do–'

'If you'd just have patience and keep your pretty mouth shut for a few minutes, I can explain everything,' Beatrice Billings sneered. Ken gripped Sally's hand.

'Let her talk,' he whispered. 'It's all evidence...'

'Boyd Wilcot wasn't interested in your father's mine ... he wanted the *surrounding land!* The purchase of the mine was just a convenient smokescreen for his *real* purpose...'

'*Now* I get it!' Ken breathed. 'Wilcot knew that Wells Fargo stolen gold was buried in a cavern under the pastureland near to the mine.' He flashed Sally a quick glance. 'That's where we emerged from underground last night.' He frowned at their captive. 'But you told us that Wilcot's father never told his son anything about the loot.'

'He didn't. But Wilcot discovered Grandpa's letter tucked inside the old family Bible.' The woman laughed harshly. 'Boyd Wilcot wasn't the religious type, so he'd never even looked at it in the twenty years since his father died. It was hidden away in a drawer and it wasn't until he moved it one day, intending to throw it out, that he discovered the letter...' Again she laughed. 'He only found it the day after he'd decided to kill Jack Andrews and frame old man Farraday for the crime. Then when he discovered that there was gold under Farraday's land, he realized that he needed him alive, to sign it over to him, without creating any suspicion. So he changed his plans accordingly.'

'The cunning, devious swine!' Ken shook his head. 'It all fits ... except for one thing: how come *you* know so much about things? How could you know? You didn't buy his land and move here until quite recently – long after Wilcot's death. You never met him at the time...'

'Oh, but I *did* meet him!' Beatrice Billings chuckled. 'After his arrest, Boyd Wilcot knew he was finished, but he had one last card still to play. He had his lawyer write to me, his only living relative, and ask me to come and see him. He told me to come veiled, so nobody would connect us afterwards.'

'I remember now!' Sally said, with a glance at Ken. 'There *was* a woman who came to see Wilcot before he was hanged. Someone told me as much, but it didn't seem important at the time–'

'It was very important,' Beatrice Billings snapped. 'Boyd told me everything that had happened. He was a pretty shrewd judge of character. They say that hereditary tendencies skip a generation. He saw that I was as tough as my grandpa, and I told him too that, to my way of thinking, I was perfectly entitled – as his granddaughter – to benefit from that outlaw legacy. In return for my promising to act as his instrument of vengeance, Wilcot told me what was in the letter, how the gold was cached underground near to the Grey Face Mine...'

'Told you?' Ken queried. 'Then he didn't give you the letter?'

'Of course not – he'd been stripped and searched before he was jailed, and the letter would have been found. He'd already destroyed it soon after he was arrested. But he gave me a description of the approximate location of the gold, where it was buried under your land.'

'But not the tunnel entrance leading to it from the mountain foothills?'

Beatrice Billings compressed her lips. 'That was the unfortunate part. He didn't know it! He knew there *was* a secret tunnel, because it was referred to in my grandfather's letter, but its precise location was not given in the letter; but was shown on a map drawing attached to it. But that fool Carl Wilcot had destroyed the map! *He'd only kept the letter!*' The woman gave a bitter glance at Ken before continuing. 'I knew you'd never agree to sell freely after all your earlier experiences, and especially after having rebuilt the ranch from scratch. So I tried to get rid of you, mainly so that your wife would be so utterly demoralized afterwards, that buying from her would be an easy proposition.'

'Only it wasn't,' Sally said, with a triumphant grin.

'Uh-huh.' The woman admitted, sighing. 'Evidently Tin Pan knew about the tunnel, but I preferred to kill him and prevent him giving you the information, even if I did lose it myself.'

Ken was looking thoughtful. 'How come it was nearly the best part of a year before you arrived as the new owner of the Treble Circle? Why didn't you take over straight away?'

'Kyle Endicott handled the conveyance and legalities. Boyd Wilcot introduced him to me at the jail – as his defending lawyer he was entitled to be there – and he told us there was a good chance that as a convicted murderer, his Treble Circle might likely be seized by the state, and then put up for auction. Naturally, the plan required me to have the ranch. Accordingly we had to take Endicott partly into our confidence. Wilcot had him draw up a fake Will, purportedly made by his father, stating that in the event of his son's death after inheriting it from him, the ranch should pass to me. Endicott knew nothing about the gold, of course. He just thought he was helping Wilcot's dying wish to have the ranch pass to a member of his family. I paid him enough to keep his mouth shut about it, too.' The woman paused, smiling faintly.

'Even so, it took Endicott nearly a year to sort out the legal formalities. I didn't mind, as it gave me time to sell my own ranch, and gather together a band of reliable men who could work for me here.'

'You mean outlaws like yourself,' Ken snapped. 'The jiggers that fired our ranch and tried to kill me.'

Beatrice Billings gave a little shrug and smiled mockingly.

Sally looked at the woman, her eyes narrowed. 'What did you mean just now by "instrument of vengeance"?'

'Surely that's obvious? Boyd Wilcot hated your so-clever husband for the way he'd tricked him. He *loathed* him, and wanted him to suffer in exactly the same way as he had. He told me about the stunt you'd pulled with the markings on his bullets. After my first attempt to kill him failed, I had the idea of pulling the same stunt on him, using his switched gun for the shooting of Tin Pan. Poetic justice! Bradmore should have been hanged after that, only...'

'Like grandfather, like granddaughter,' Sally misquoted. 'All right, we've heard enough. This means you're going to the sheriff right now, Mrs Billings–'

'Oh no, she ain't!' a voice snapped from the doorway, and Ken and Sally both twirled round.

'Drop your guns,' commanded the lean puncher in the Stetson, who came forward. 'I mean it, Bradmore,' he added; 'or your wife'll get one in th' belly.' Ken dropped his gun with a clatter and Sally did likewise. The pair of them raised their arms.

'Good work, Jed,' Beatrice Billings commented approvingly, fingering her still-smarting cheek.

'I figgered there was somethin' wrong when in makin' my reg'lar night check-up I found the screen door abusted,' the Treble Circle foreman said.

Beatrice Billings nodded, smiling grimly. 'As I knew you would – which is why I kept these two talking...' Suddenly she whipped round her hand and gave Sally a vicious back-hander across the face which knocked her flying into a chair.

'A little on account,' the woman explained

coldly. 'And now I'll tell you what I'm going to do. I'm going to shoot the pair of you – and shoot to kill. Then I'll have the bullets extracted – to destroy evidence if you're ever found – and have your bodies sealed up in that cave. I don't think you'll ever be found. At the same time I'll have the gold removed to a spot where a go-between is waiting to pay me cash for it.'

Ken glanced quickly about him, and back at the two guns – the foreman's trained on him, and Beatrice Billings' on Sally. He noted the position of the two gunhands – then with all the power at his command he jumped, arms outflung.

He acted so abruptly that neither the foreman or Beatrice had the chance to fire their weapons. With his last vestiges of strength, his right arm slammed down on their two forearms, knocking the guns spinning. With his left he delivered an uppercut that hurtled the foreman into the wall. The foreman used the wall to spring himself back again, delivering a vicious body jab that keeled Ken backwards. Both men ignoring their weapons, they slammed savagely into each other.

For a second or two Beatrice Billings was caught off guard – but not Sally. She dived out of her chair to the gun the woman had dropped, then she yelled as the woman's fingers tore into her thick hair and dragged her backwards.

'No you don't!' she snapped; but, despite the pain of being half-scalped, Sally seized the woman's ankles and pulled with all her strength, crashing the woman down on her back.

Ken, in his weakened state, was too occupied in protecting himself to notice what the two women were doing, but Sally's shriek did divert his attention for a moment and it lost him his initial advantage. The foreman's fist struck him a mighty blow in the jaw. Blinding lights blazed through his skull as he blundered on to the table, sagged across it, and collapsed helplessly on the other side.

Sally reached the gun, turned and fired. The foreman gasped, gripping his arm tightly as the bullet tore flesh. Sally gazed at him, debating whether to fire another shot. She suddenly found the gun whirled from her by Beatrice.

Dazed, Ken watched events as the woman backed to the open doorway, the foreman at her side clutching his wounded shoulder.

'All either of you have done is delay

things,' she said bitterly. 'I still mean to kill you – and to do it now. I'll take you first, Mrs Bradmore, since you like to think yourself so tough!'

Ken watched helplessly, knowing he could never make another effort to save the situation. Sally, dishevelled and breathing hard, stood by the table, staring at the gun in fascination...

Then suddenly there were three shots in rapid succession, but not from Beatrice Billings' weapon. They came from the hall behind her. A blank expression crossed her face and the gun fell from her hand. Gradually she sagged and fell flat.

Astounded, the foreman whirled round and dived into the hall, to meet another two bullets. He staggered, halted, and fell on his knees. Then he tumbled over and remained still.

Silence. Ken slowly crept forward to the gun the woman had dropped. He yanked it up and levelled it into the dark hall.

'Whoever you are, come out of there!' he commanded, motioning Sally to get out of range.

He knew he was taking a risk, that whoever was out there in the dark could probably fire point blank – but he chanced it. To his surprise his command was obeyed and into the room there came the stooped, shifty-eyed ex-servant, Axia.

'Mean no harm, Mr Bradmore – or lady,' he said, shrugging and handing over his .45. 'Settle account. Said I would kill Miss Alland for what she did to me. I did jus' in time.'

'Yeah – just in time is right,' Ken agreed, straightening up. 'Keep him covered, Sal,' he added, as she picked up her own Colt.

He moved to where the foreman and woman were lying, examining them quickly.

'Dead – both of 'em,' he announced. 'Listen, you...' He swung on the half-breed. 'I'm goin' to need you to explain this lot to th' sheriff, otherwise he's goin' to think my wife and I did this...'

Ken broke off at the sound of footfalls in the hall. He cocked his gun in readiness, then gave a start of surprise as the sheriff himself came into view, two of his burly deputies behind him.

'I reckon you've nothin' to explain, Ken,' Garson said quietly. 'I saw what happened.'

'You did? But, what brings you here, anyway?'

'This guy Axia.' Garson gave the half-breed a grim look. 'He came to my office this evening, plainly bent on makin' trouble, an' said he'd noticed that among Miss Alland's steers there was a lot of 'em with altered brands, some of 'em bein' *your* brand. I could tell he was tellin' me t'get revenge on Miss Alland – or is it Mrs Billings? – for kickin' him off the spread. So I agreed to ride over to ask her a few questions...'

'You said tomorrow morning!' the half-breed shouted angrily.

'Yeah,' Garson agreed laconically. 'I'd plumb forgotten that among other things tomorrow I've a journey outa town to make. So I came t'night and landed just in time to hear, then see this little fracas, but too late to stop it. I reckon you're in the clear, Ken, and you too, Mrs Bradmore. Take this jigger out, boys,' he added, nodding to the halfbreed.

Struggling uselessly the ex-servant was dragged away. The sheriff looked down thoughtfully at the bodies.

'They'll have to be moved,' he said. 'Funny how things work out sometimes... That half-breed 'd never have come on the prod as he did had he thought I'd be around tonight... But look, what's it all *about?* I can't figger it.'

'It's simple enough,' Sally said urgently. 'It concerns some Wells Fargo stolen gold.'

'Yeah?' Garson gave her a sharp look and Ken took up the story in detail. It left the sheriff reflective.

'So *that*'s where that fortune in stolen gold went, was it? Bin on my list of missing stuff for long enough – and on the files of my predecessors in office.'

'And of course you'll take it away?' Sally asked, with a wistful smile. 'It can't be called salvage or anything?'

'Nope, it's, government property. Even if it was salvage you don't own the land no more where it's buried... But I'll tell you this much,' Garson added, grinning, 'there's bin a standin' government reward of a hundred thousand dollars for long enough, for anybody givin' information leadin' to its recovery. You've sure given it!'

'A – a hundred thousand!' Sally gave a gulp and stared at Ken. 'Ken, with that we could–'

'Buy our land back, *and* the ranches of the other two as well.' Ken hugged her in delight. 'Since nobody owns 'em any more, them leavin' no issue, they're state property, aren't they, Sheriff?'

'Sure are,' he acknowledged. 'An' I reckon

they'll be goin' mighty cheap ... but say,' he added, 'how are you two goin' to manage three spreads?'

'I'm goin' to offer one to my sister and Bill Winslow, and their boy, William junior—'

'An' the other?'

Sally put her arms around Ken's neck, and looked at the sheriff over his shoulder.

She winked.

This Large Print Book, for people
who cannot read normal print,
is published under the auspices of

THE ULVERSCROFT FOUNDATION

... we hope you have enjoyed this book.
Please think for a moment about those
who have worse eyesight than you ...
and are unable to even read or enjoy
Large Print without great difficulty.

You can help them by sending a
donation, large or small, to:

**The Ulverscroft Foundation,
1, The Green, Bradgate Road,
Anstey, Leicestershire, LE7 7FU,
England.**
or request a copy of our brochure for
more details.

The Foundation will use all donations
to assist those people who are visually
impaired and need special attention
with medical research, diagnosis
and treatment.

Thank you very much for your help.